"It's Late.

"No!" Sara's cry so... ...almost involuntary. "I—I mean, you don't have to. You could…stay."

There was no mistaking her meaning. Her face was suffused with the delicate flush of passion, the glow of a woman waiting, willing to be loved. He'd never realized that desire could be such a pure and simple thing, almost holy when shining from a pair of deep blue eyes.

She was offering him everything he hungered for, and he didn't know why he didn't just reach out and take advantage of it. She was his gypsy lady. All the warmth that had always been missing from his black-and-white world.

He hesitated one moment more before taking the biggest risk of his life.

Mike Parker reached out of the shadows and took Sara's hand.

Dear Reader,

A sexy fire fighter, a crazy cat and a dynamite heroine—that's what you'll find in *Lucy and the Loner*, Elizabeth Bevarly's wonderful MAN OF THE MONTH. It's the next in her installment of THE FAMILY McCORMICK series, and it's also a MAN OF THE MONTH book you'll never forget—warm, humorous and very sexy!

A story from Lass Small is always a delight, and *Chancy's Cowboy* is Lass at her most marvelous. Don't miss out as Chancy decides to take some lessons in love from a handsome hunk of a cowboy!

Eileen Wilks's latest, *The Wrong Wife*, is chock-full with the sizzling tension and compelling reading that you've come to expect from this rising Desire star. And so many of you know and love Barbara McCauley that she needs no introduction, but this month's *The Nanny and the Reluctant Rancher* is sure to both please her current fans…and win her new readers!

Suzannah Davis is another new author that we're excited about, and *Dr. Holt and the Texan* may just be her best book to date! And the month is completed with a delightful romp from Susan Carroll, *Parker and the Gypsy*.

There's something for everyone. So come and relish the romantic variety you've come to expect from Silhouette Desire!

Lucia Macro

Lucia Macro
And the Editors at Silhouette Desire

Please address questions and book requests to:
Silhouette Reader Service
U.S.: 3010 Walden Ave., P.O. Box 1325, Buffalo, NY 14269
Canadian: P.O. Box 609, Fort Erie, Ont. L2A 5X3

SUSAN CARROLL
PARKER AND THE GYPSY

SILHOUETTE *Desire*®
Published by Silhouette Books
America's Publisher of Contemporary Romance

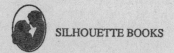 SILHOUETTE BOOKS

ISBN 0-373-76068-X

PARKER AND THE GYPSY

Books by Susan Carroll

Silhouette Desire

Black Lace and Linen #840
Love Power #876
Parker and the Gypsy #1068

SUSAN CARROLL

began her career by writing Regency romances. It was a long way from the starch of the British aristocracy to the sizzle of a contemporary American love story. But, in making the leap, Susan found one thing remained the same: that spark of humor that gives zest to any romance, no matter what the time period.

Susan draws on the same humor in her own life. Currently residing in Illinois, she keeps busy between books, coping with two lively children, two rambunctious cats and one very noisy hamster.

To my friend Paula Jolly, for reading the runes and helping to keep my aura fluffed.

One

Mikey ran through the maze of dark alleys, heart thumping beneath his ragged T-shirt, his grubby sneakers pounding the cold, hard concrete. Behind the kid, the shadow of a man loomed, tall and wavering in the streetlights, like a dangling spider.

Mikey glanced wildly about him for an escape route, but there was none. Brick walls enclosed him on all four sides. A ragged sob tore from his chest as he whirled about. The shadow man crept closer, ever closer. The boy flattened himself against the wall, tears streaking down his dirty cheeks as his stalker stepped into the light.

Mikey could almost see his face now....

"No! Go away," the boy screamed as the shadow-man grabbed at him, his fingers sinking into Mikey's shoulder like bony talons. With his other hand, the dark demon raised his knife—

"No!"

The word tore from Mike Parker's throat as he wrenched awake, his head snapping back against the battered upholstery of his office chair. The leather creaked as he sat bolt upright and clenched the sides of his old oak desk, his brown eyes flying wide open. It took a few moments for him to remember where he was. The four plaster walls, the steel file cabinets and other trappings of his one man detective agency slowly penetrated his sleep-fogged brain.

No dark alleys. No shadow man. No knife. He had just dozed off at his desk, had a bad dream. That was all. But for a brief second, Mike felt all of twelve years old again. Small, helpless and scared. His hand crept reflexively to his shoulder, seeking traces of the wound that had long ago healed. Or should have. Damp patches stained the black T-shirt that hugged the hard contours of his chest, but they were from perspiration, not blood.

Swearing under his breath, Mike shook his head in disgust, raking back uneven lengths of tawny-colored hair from his eyes.

At the age of thirty four, he was too old for this, to be still having nightmares about the bogeyman. Or in this case, a *day-mare*. Anytime he was overtired or a little run-down, he could almost count on that stupid dream to come creeping up on him again. But after all these years, why, damn it?

"The answer is obvious, Michael," the grad student from Rutgers he'd once dated had told him. "The dream is a manifest sign about some unresolved issue from your childhood."

"You don't say," Mike had snapped, wondering how they'd gotten around to discussing his restless sleep habits in the first place. He'd been quick to change the subject with a suggestive remark that had brought both the uncomfortable conversation and his dinner date with the lovely Carolyn Saunders to an abrupt end. As she had stormed out of the restaurant, Mike had resolved upon two things. In the future, to steer clear of women who called him Michael. And to keep his dreams to himself.

"Manifest sign," he muttered, still irritated by the memory of Carolyn's attempts to play Sigmund Freud. The *issues* of his childhood had all been resolved quite well as far as he was concerned. Locked neatly away behind the bars of Trenton State Prison and forgotten.

The only thing the damn dream was ever a sign of was a hangover, just like the one that was making his head pound this morning. The dull pain still throbbed behind his eyes despite the cold shower and aspirin tablets that had gotten him awake and into his office earlier that morning.

Rummaging around in his top desk drawer, Mike managed to locate the plastic bottle and shook out two more white tablets into his hand. Uncoiling his six-foot-two frame from the chair, he dragged himself over to the water cooler and filled a stained ceramic coffee cup. He gagged down both aspirin in one huge gulp.

The blasted air-conditioning was on the fritz again and outside his open second story window, the heat and noisy traffic of another Atlantic City summer morning assaulted his much-battered senses in one great oppressive wave. He couldn't remember how much he'd had to drink last night, but if it had him dreaming about the shadow man again, it had obviously been too much.

It had all started out harmlessly enough—hefting a few cool ones at Boom Boom's Bar and Grill with his friend Jimmy Potts, in celebration of Jimmy's upcoming marriage. Mike had spent most of the time staring morosely into his glass and wondering how many months it would take before Jimmy turned up in his office, hiring Mike to get the goods on the little woman when she took to cheating with some new Romeo. That, in Mike's bitter experience, was how most marital bliss panned out. All those hearts and flowers, promises of love and eternal devotion—just another con game.

Despite his raging headache, Mike congratulated himself on surviving this bachelor party better than he had the last one, when he'd trailed after the girl who'd jumped out of the cake. Darcy Robbins. But she was another nightmare he'd just as soon forget.

Rubbing one hand along his unshaven jaw, Mike tried to summon up the energy to return to his desk and complete the report he'd been working on before he'd fallen asleep. Skip traces on some missing deadbeats for a local finance company. Boring as hell but—

A knock sounded on his office door, nearly startling him into dropping the coffee cup. As he replaced the mug back on top of the water cooler, he grumbled, "Now what?"

He knew it couldn't be his secretary. Rosa had no respect for a closed door. She barged in whenever she felt like it. The rapping sounded again, causing Mike to wince. "All right, all right!" he snarled. "Just stop the damn pounding and come in."

The door opened slowly and Mike blinked at the vision that filled his threshold. It was as though a burst of sunlight had pierced his gloom-ridden office and assumed the form of a woman. She was all softness, from the rainbow-hued skirt that clung to the willowy outline of her hips, to the white flowing blouse that shifted half off her creamy shoulders.

Golden ringlets rioted about a heart-shaped face with features as delicate as fine porcelain, from the dainty nose to the small determined chin. She regarded Mike with the most wistful blue eyes he'd ever seen.

She had an angel's hair, an angel's eyes, an angel's mouth. It took Mike a moment to realize he wasn't breathing and to exhale deeply. It took him a moment longer to snap back to his senses and remember that the only angels he had any use for were the fallen kind.

This young woman had that look of dewy-eyed innocence about her that usually meant nothing but trouble. When she hesitated, fretting her lip, Mike barked out, "What can I do for you, sis? Are you sure you've got the right office? The Save-a-Soul Mission's on the first floor."

"I'm not looking for the mission," she said softly.

She had an angel's voice, too. Mike grimaced.

"I'm looking for Michael Parker."

"You've found him."

"Oh, no!" Her mouth dropped open in dismay. She took a cautious step closer, her remarkable blue eyes traveling over him. "I—I mean you just can't be Mr. Parker."

"I forget a lot of things the morning after I've tied one

on," Mike said with a sardonic lift of one brow, "but I gen-
erally manage to remember my name."

"I'm sorry." A flush rose into her cheeks. "I guess I do
see the resemblance now."

Her shoulders sagged as disbelief appeared to give way to
disappointment, but Mike was used to that. He'd been disap-
pointing people all his life—his high school teachers, his foster
parents, his ex-wife....

The woman's gaze flicked from Mike to the newspaper she
held clutched in her hand. "It's just that you don't look very
much like your picture."

Closing the distance between them, Mike snatched the paper
away to see just what she had there. It was a puff piece about
him, inserted in the *Golden Times Gazette,* a weekly magazine
distributed mostly to local retirement communities, written and
edited by Mrs. Eudora Jenkins, a very grateful former client
of his. A more glowing testimonial about the Parker Agency
could hardly have been penned by his own grandmother.

Mike didn't know what was worse: the glaring headline,
Mike Parker, Crusading P.I., or the sappy photograph that ac-
companied the article. He would have been hard-pressed to
recognize himself from the picture, his broad shoulders encased in a tuxedo, his slightly crooked mouth angled into a
debonair smile.

Mike thrust the paper back at the woman who had invaded
his office. "I was doing undercover work," he explained.

"Oh!" Her brow cleared. "You mean you were on a stake-
out last night. That explains...everything." Her gaze drifted
over his disheveled appearance.

No, it didn't, Mike wanted to argue. What he'd meant was
that he'd been doing undercover work when he'd been all
trussed up in that tuxedo. His present appearance—the beat-
up sneakers, the faded jeans, the T-shirt—was much closer to
his natural state.

But somehow he couldn't bring himself to tell her that. Not
with her beaming at him that way, with such a radiant smile.

She had an angel's smile...

He caught himself wishing that he had at least taken time

to shave after his quick shower. Finger combing his hair in a self-conscious gesture, Mike cleared his throat. "I don't usually see walk-ins. But if you'd like to step out in the reception room and set up an appointment with my secretary—"

"But she isn't there."

Mike stepped around her to peer into the outer office. She was right. Rosa's desk was empty. She had never come in to work.

"Damn! She's probably planning to call in sick again," he said. "Off to visit Dr. Blackjack at the United Memorial Casino."

When his visitor regarded him blankly, Mike explained, "That's a joke."

"Oh." Again that blinding smile.

It galvanized Mike into stalking forward and pulling up one of the seasick green vinyl chairs that comprised his office decor. He couldn't remember when the last time was he'd leapt to hold a chair for any woman, but he was doing it now.

"As long as you're here," he said, "you might as well sit down."

"Thank you." She sank gracefully onto the seat. As Mike pushed the chair into place before his desk, he experienced a double assault on his senses. First the sight of her slim, shapely legs as she crossed them. Then the exotic scent that seemed to radiate from the golden cloud of her hair.

The sweet perfume rendered him a little dizzy. Or maybe, he told himself, it was still the effect of last night's excesses. He stumbled back to his own seat behind the desk and tried to look nonchalant, leaning back in his chair.

"So what can I do for you?"

"Well, Mr. Parker—"

"Please. Mr. Parker was my father." Or at least it was until the old man traded his name for the number stamped across his prison inmate's uniform. Mike shoved the grim thought aside before adding, "Call me 'Mike.'"

"Mike," she repeated, her smile gone suddenly shy. Her golden-tipped lashes drifted down. "It's very hard for me to know where to begin."

"Then why don't we start with something easy? Like *your* name."

"It's Sara Holyfield. And no *h*. In Sara, that is."

"Sara with no *h*," Mike murmured, but he was distracted by the silvery glint of her earrings. To his complete fascination, he saw that she was wearing naked fairies dangling off each ear. Very nubile fairies with delicate wings.

And there appeared to be another one suspended from a chain around her neck. This creature poised on top of some kind of crystal. Mike started to lean forward, tracing the path of the fairy where it danced down the front of her blouse, but he caught himself just in time.

Shoving aside the stack of paper that littered his desk—several days' worth of unopened mail—Mike attempted to assume a more professional stance. He managed to locate a notepad and a pen that actually worked. Jotting down Sara's name, he pressed her for a few more basic facts such as her address and phone number.

"Aurora Falls, New Jersey, huh?" he commented as he scrawled the information on his pad. "You drove a long way to find yourself a detective."

"There was no one back there who could help me."

"Suppose you tell me what the problem is and I'll see what I can do."

Sara nodded, but she still appeared reluctant to proceed. Mike had encountered this before in first-time clients—the nervousness, the embarrassment to talk of what were often highly personal difficulties. Usually he lost patience and ordered his customers to cut to the chase.

But something about Sara Holyfield inspired an unaccustomed gentleness in him. Mike tried to set her at her ease by offering her a piece of his favorite peppermint gum. When she declined, he popped a stick in his own mouth, then settled back in his chair with what he hoped was a father-confessor type of expression.

"Just relax and take your time," he soothed.

She started to speak and ended up fretting with her purse strings instead. She had smooth graceful fingers with neat, well-trimmed nails—nothing like those red-painted talons his ex-wife, Darcy, had sported. Mike had a notion Sara's hands would feel all warm and silky, just like the rest of her ivory-toned skin.

He clicked the peppermint gum against his teeth, annoyed that he had let his mind go skipping off like that again. After an awkward silence, he probed delicately, "There's some trouble with your husband perhaps?"

She shook her head vigorously, the fairies swinging with her hair. "I've never been married."

"A boyfriend, then?"

"He's moved to Texas."

"And you want me to trace him?"

"No." Her lips quirked in a wry half smile. "I assure you I don't want him found."

"Good! I mean, that's too bad. I mean—" Hell, Mike wasn't sure what he meant or why this woman was unnerving him so. Maybe it was because he could usually peg any client within minutes after they'd walked in the door, guess what they wanted before they ever opened their mouths.

But he wasn't able to do that with her. He didn't have a clue why she was there. Angels shouldn't have problems, should they? But something was sure distressing this one. Beyond that serene exterior, he could see it in her eyes. A deep-rooted sadness. If his heart hadn't been made of shoe leather, it would have moved even him.

"I suppose I should start by telling you a little more about myself," she said at last. She stood up and paced restlessly to the window. The sunlight filtering through the blinds haloed her hair and rendered her white cotton blouse almost transparent.

"Have you ever had a revelation, Mr. Parker?" she asked.

"No," Mike croaked. But he was having one now. She wasn't wearing a bra. He could see the shadow of her small, full breasts quite clearly, down to the pert outline of her nipples.

His response was swift, inevitable and very male. Chewing his gum furiously, Mike forced himself to look away. This surge of attraction was unprofessional, but he couldn't seem to help it. The life of a private detective was far from glamorous. It was pretty mundane most of the time. After months of pot-bellied men and little old ladies coming through his door, no wonder he was jolted by the sight of a beautiful young woman.

It was like something out of one of those hokey old detective movies that he had a sneaking fondness for. The mysterious dame swishes into the gumshoe's office, innocent, but alluring, begging for his help.

There would be danger, hairbreadth escapes. Of course, he'd eventually save her life and she would be terribly grateful. Mike got to the point in his imaginings where Miss Sara Holyfield was demonstrating some of that gratitude, slipping that soft blouse off her even-softer shoulders, guiding his hands toward her—

Whoa! This ridiculous fantasy wasn't doing anything to help his—er—condition. He actually felt beads of sweat gathering on his brow. Sara had finally started talking and he'd hardly registered a word of it.

"…and I realized I'd been wasting my life and talents. After I received the inheritance from my great-aunt Marilla, I walked out of my job at the bank and never looked back. I went to work for myself the very next day."

Mike risked a peek at her. Mercifully she had stepped out of the revealing pool of sunlight. He didn't know whether he was more relieved or disappointed.

She turned slowly to face him. "Which brings me to why I'm here. I need to hire you to collaborate with me on a case."

Mike blinked. Boy, he must have really missed something when he'd been daydreaming. "*You* are a detective?"

"Of a sort." Her chin tipped up a notch in an attitude that could have been pride or defiance. "I'm a psychic investigator."

Mike swallowed his gum and damn near choked. "You— you mean like—like a ghost buster?"

"I don't bust ghosts, Mr. Parker. I merely explore evidence of supernatural phenomenon."

"Oh, is *that* all?"

"I also run a New Age book store and do psychic readings."

Mike stared at her. She stared back, looking as calm as if she'd just told him she was a dental hygienist. He expelled his breath in a long sigh. Great. He'd finally gotten his alluring, mysterious dame, and with his usual luck, she turned out to be a nut case. Or else she was planning to pull off some incredible hustle on him. Life was so damned unfair.

Swiveling glumly back to the desk, he said, "Sorry, Miss Holyfield, but I don't think I can help you. I always confine my investigations to this side of the grave."

"I don't expect you to go ghost hunting with me, if that's what you're afraid of. I have no trouble with that."

"I'll bet," Mike mumbled under his breath.

Bracing her hands upon his desk, she leaned forward. Mike was assaulted again by the scent of her perfume, the soft rise and fall of her breasts.

What a waste. He stifled a groan.

She peered down at him earnestly. "I'm sorry. I'm afraid I haven't been making myself all that clear. I'm here on behalf of a Miss Mamie Patrick. She's trying to find her son."

"Oh. A missing-persons case. Why didn't you say so to begin with? That's different. That's—" *Normal* Mike almost added. It wasn't the first time someone like this Patrick woman was misguided or desperate enough to consult a psychic to recover their missing child. Mike wasn't sure he wanted to get mixed-up in this business. But his interest was piqued enough to reach for his notepad again.

"Okay, sit down," he said to Sara. "And this time give it to me straight without the psychic bull—that is, just give me the cold, hard facts."

Sara sank back into her chair, folding her hands primly. "Well, Mamie—Miss Patrick—first made contact with me about two weeks ago. Her only son, John Francis, was put up for adoption when he was six years old. For her own peace of mind, she desperately needs to see him again."

Mike noted the name of the Patrick kid on his pad. "And how long has it been since she last saw the boy?"

"John Patrick would be somewhere in his late thirties by now." Sara added anxiously, "Do you think there's any real hope that you can find him after all this time, Mr. Parker?"

"Anything's possible. Although I have to warn you, adoption records in New Jersey are sealed." Mike shrugged. "I'll have to talk to this Miss Patrick myself and see what leads she can give me, but frankly, I think you should make sure she really wants this matter pursued. These tender family reunions you watch on the talk shows are not always what they're cracked up to be. After all this time, Mamie Patrick might be better off forgetting about her son and getting on with her life."

"That would be difficult," Sara said quietly. "She's dead."

"What!" Mike pressed down so hard with the pen, he punctured the paper.

"Mamie Patrick died over thirty years ago."

"You mean...you're telling me this client of yours is—is a—"

"A supernatural manifestation."

"Let's use plain English here. You mean a ghost."

"Well...yes."

"Ah, jeez!" Mike ripped off the sheet of notebook paper he'd been filling out and crumpled it into a ball that he arced into his metal waste can. Shoving to his feet, he stalked around the desk.

Sara shrank back, looking mildly alarmed as Mike's hands closed around her arms. He tugged her to her feet.

"Mr. Parker! Mike, what—what are you doing?"

"It's not what I'm doing, doll. It's what you're doing. Leaving."

He started hustling her toward the door, but Sara dug in her heels. "What's the matter? Have I said something wrong?"

Mike rolled his eyes. "No, nothing much. You just waltzed in here and asked me to go to work for some woman who kicked the bucket over a quarter of a century ago."

"Oh, so that's it." Sara managed to wriggle free of his

grasp. She angled a challenging glance up at him. "You don't believe in ghosts?"

"No, I sure as hell don't."

"But you just said a moment ago that anything's possible."

"I meant anything *normal,* not things that go bump in the night. I don't believe in anything that I can't see, hear, smell or feel."

"Then that means that you don't believe in intuition. Or faith. Or even love." She exuded a soft sigh. "That's very sad."

"Yeah, tragic." She was the one ready for a straitjacket and yet she had the nerve to stand there looking as though she felt sorry for him.

Stepping around her, he swung open the door. "Sorry I can't be of service, but I'm sure you and Miss Patrick will manage just swell without me. Maybe you can locate the guy in your crystal ball."

"I don't have a crystal ball," Sara said reproachfully. "If I had that much psychic power, I wouldn't need you to help Mamie."

"If she's a ghost, why doesn't Miss Mamie just fly off and find the kid herself?"

"She's restricted to the old Pine Top Inn, the last place she lived before she died. Manifestations usually cannot go wherever they want to."

"Ghosts have rules?"

"Everyone has rules, Mr. Parker."

"And one of mine happens to be I don't take on any client where I have to hold a séance to present my bill. So if you don't mind—" Mike indicated the door with a sweeping gesture, but Sara ignored him, fishing inside her purse instead.

"If you're worried about being paid, you needn't be," she said. "I can write you a check right now."

Mike pressed one hand to his brow. This woman just wasn't getting the message. As she started to drag out her checkbook, he covered her hand to stop her.

"Look, honey, save your dough. I have a feeling you're

going to need it. Good psychiatric care is expensive these days.''

She flinched as though he'd struck her ''I was hoping that you would be much more open-minded, Mr. Parker.''

''Whatever gave you an idea like that?''

''It was your picture in the paper. Your face...it seemed so wise and accepting. And kind.''

''That was my dazed look. A flashbulb had just gone off in my eyes.''

''But I was so certain you were the one to help,'' Sara murmured almost to herself. ''I could sense it, and when I trust my instincts, I'm almost never wrong.''

Pressing her lips in a stubborn line, she gazed up at Mike again. ''Would you mind letting me feel your aura?''

''Feel my what?'' Mike's pulses rioted with the possibilities. But it was only his hand she reached for. She turned it palm upward.

He tugged free of her grasp, but she begged, ''Please. Just let me run this one little test. Then I promise I'll go away and leave you alone.''

Mike opened his mouth to argue, then closed it again as she looked up at him, pleading. Why was he always such a sucker for big blue eyes?

Grimacing, he held out his hand. ''This test isn't going to involve voodoo pins or anything like that?''

''Of course not.'' She cupped his hand in her own smaller fragile one. ''Now close your eyes.''

''What for?'' he asked suspiciously.

''I'm not going to hurt you. Trust me.''

It had been a damned long time since Mike had trusted anyone, but he gave a long-suffering sigh and shut his eyes. She ran her fingertips lightly across his open palm.

''Just relax, Mr. Parker.''

Mike sucked in his breath. That wasn't what was going to happen if she kept stroking him in that slow, sensual fashion. When her soft fingers danced across his wrist, his pulse gave an erratic leap. He was starting to really enjoy this when, to his disappointment, she stopped.

"Now I'm going to close my eyes and lower my hand toward yours. If we do this right, as I get closer, you should feel a surge of power between us."

"This is stupid," Mike grumbled. He wished she'd go back to the caressing part again. He felt like a total idiot standing here with his hand held out like a bellboy hoping for a tip.

"Please, Mr. Parker. Concentrate and keep your eyes closed."

Mike tried to, but he'd always had the same problem not peeking whenever he played hide-and-seek as a kid. He cracked one eye open and realized that whatever else Sara might be, she wasn't a con artist. She really believed in all this mumbo jumbo.

Her smooth brow was furrowed in earnest concentration. Her purse balanced in her left hand, her right one hovered barely an inch above his own. There was something strangely arousing about standing so close to her, just short of touching. He had only to reach out to bury his fingers in her ripples of silky gold hair, trace the line of that fairy chain along the smooth white column of her throat.

With her eyes closed, a delicate flush coloring her cheeks, she almost appeared as though she were in some sort of trance, like that sleeping princess in those sappy stories his one foster mom had insisted upon reading to him. If Sleeping Beauty had looked anything like Sara, no wonder that dopey prince had risked burning his a—fighting dragons to get to her bedroom.

"Are you experiencing anything yet, Mr. Parker?" she asked.

"Not a blessed thing," Mike denied, but he was disturbed to notice his hand begin to tremble. A tingling sensation started in his fingertips, quickly spreading along his arm, through the rest of his body to become the most intoxicating rush of desire he'd ever known.

Sara's eyes fluttered open to stare straight into his. She frowned. "You haven't really been trying. Didn't you feel any impulse at all?"

Mike shook his head. Oh, he was having plenty of impulses all right, but none, he feared, that Sara would approve of.

"Let's try it again," he murmured. "Close your eyes."

She looked a little wary, but obeyed. She stood before him, her lips half-parted in unconscious invitation. This was too easy, Mike thought with a groan. He should be ashamed of himself. He should resist the temptation, but he didn't seem able to help himself.

Bending forward, he covered her mouth with his own. He felt Sara stiffen with surprise, but then he was a little surprised himself. He'd never kissed any woman this gently before. At least, it started out that way.

But when Sara didn't resist, he folded her in his arms, deepening the embrace. She tasted and felt just like she smelled— all softness, innocence and seduction. He kissed her with increasing hunger, passion and heat rushing through him, warming places inside him that he had not even realized had gone cold.

Two

Sara clung to Mike's shoulders, his mouth wreaking havoc with her senses, even her sixth one. Since she'd set foot in the door, this interview had gone nothing like she'd anticipated. Not only had Mike Parker turned out to be more rough-edged than she'd expected, he was now kissing her in a way to make her curls stand on end.

Any protest she should have voiced was swept away beneath the hot mastery of Mike's lips on hers. Her purse dropped from her nerveless fingers, hitting the carpet with a soft thud. She melted closer, her head reeling. Her mind felt like she was floating, her body like it was on fire.

It was only when his tongue breached her lips, exploring her mouth with even greater intimacy, that alarm set in. Struggling to be free, she insinuated her hands between them, breaking off the heated contact of their mouths.

His breathing ragged, Mike blinked at her. For a moment, he looked as dazed as she felt. She had never experienced a kiss like that in her whole life. It would have been rather wonderful…if only he had really meant it.

But Mike was already making a rapid recovery. The tender set of his mouth hardened into the familiar sarcastic smirk.

"Sorry," he said. "I guess my psychic—um—gizmo got a little out of control."

Sara felt her cheeks heat, but this time with humiliation. Mike's arms were still wrapped loosely about her waist. Bracing both hands against his chest, she squirmed away from him.

"You don't have to believe in the same things I do, Mr. Parker," she said. "But you don't have to make fun of me, either."

"I wasn't making fun of you."

"Then what do you call this?" Sara raised a trembling finger to her bruised lips.

"I was kissing you." A shade of irritation crept into Mike's voice. "You can't go feeling up a guy's aura and not expect him to react."

"That wasn't the sort of reaction you were supposed to— Oh, never mind." Sara bent down to retrieve her purse from the carpet, gathering up the tattered remains of her dignity, as well. By the time she straightened, she managed to face Mike with some degree of calm.

"I'm sorry you're such an unhappy man, Mr. Parker. But that doesn't give you the right to mock and hurt other people."

"I'm not unhappy, just hung over. So if you don't mind, close the door quietly on your way out."

"I'll go," Sara said. "But that doesn't change anything. You're a miserable and lonely man with a very disturbed aura, full of bitterness and a pain that's as old as—as your wound."

"Wound?" Mike scowled at her. "What wound?"

Sara blinked as she realized the words she'd just blurted out. She stared at Mike and suddenly an image came to her of Mike's bare chest in all its glorious detail—hard-sculpted muscle from the flat plane of his stomach to the broad reach of his shoulders, smooth skin as bronzed and warm as sunlight. Except for—

"You—you have a scar on your left shoulder," Sara said haltingly.

Mike's eyes widened. "What have you got, X-ray vision or something?"

"N-no." Sara flushed, feeling as if she'd been caught sneaking peeks at Mike naked in his shower. "I *told* you I was psychic, didn't I? Sometimes these perceptions just come to me. That scar on your shoulder goes as deep as your soul, Mike Parker. It was made by something cold...something sharp." Sara shivered. "A knife perhaps? With a long—"

"Enough, already," Mike snarled, breaking her concentration. "Who the hell put you up to this?"

"Put me up to— Why, no one. I don't know what you mean."

"Either some jerk with a warped sense of humor sent you here to yank my chain or else you really are one total spook. Either way, I want you out of my office. Now!"

Sara took a hasty step back at Mike's menacing approach. "I'm sorry if I've upset you, but I assure you no one sent me. I came to you because I honestly needed your help, Mr. Parker. What am I supposed to do about finding John Patrick? If you won't take the case, could you at least—"

"Out!"

Before Sara could say another word, she found herself being roughly shoved into the tiny outer office. Mike slammed the door closed between them with a bang that was both loud and final.

"Recommend another detective?" Sara finished weakly, realizing she was addressing dead silence. She sensed that Mike Parker had just closed more doors than the one to his office. Any extrasensory perceptions she'd been having about Mike had ceased as abruptly as a phone line being disconnected.

Which was probably just as well. She'd definitely struck some kind of nerve when she'd started to probe into the mysteries of the scar on his shoulder. She'd never meant for that to happen. She tried not to invade the privacy of anyone's personal life or thoughts unless invited to do so. But she hadn't been able to help herself in Mike's case.

The vision had caught her completely unaware. It had been as exhilarating and frightening as standing on the brink of some dark chasm, unable to see what lay at the bottom, but watching a ray of light slowly starting to stretch downward. Even if Mike hadn't stopped her, Sara would have snatched herself back. Beneath his teasing wise-guy manner, she sensed something dark and disturbing about the man. She didn't want a closer look at the secrets of his mind…or his body.

"You didn't come here today to do a psychic reading or to be mentally undressing Mike Parker," she reminded herself. "You came here to hire a detective."

And in that she had just failed miserably.

Sara stole another look at Mike's closed door and issued a long sigh of frustration and disappointment.

"So what am I supposed to do now?" she murmured, sagging down dispiritedly into the office's sole waiting chair. On the secretary's desk, the phone console burred softly, the incoming call light blinking off and on. Between throwing paying customers out of his office and ignoring his phone calls, Sara wondered how Mike Parker managed to stay in business.

She thought of reaching for the battered telephone directory she saw perched on the corner of the absent Rosa's desk, thumbing through it for the listing of another private detective, but after her failure with Mike, she couldn't seem to summon up the heart to do so.

She had been just so blasted convinced that Mike would be the man to help her find Mamie's lost son. She'd already tried everything she could think of, even going so far as to insert an ad in the newspaper, asking that anyone with information on Mamie or John Patrick contact her at once. When Sara had met with no response, the sympathetic Mrs. Jenkins had suggested she hire Mike Parker, the old lady showing her the glowing article written about the man.

Sara had come to Atlantic City with high hopes, expecting to find a man with the wisdom of Sherlock Holmes, the dapperness of Hercule Poirot and the sophistication of Nick Charles all rolled into one.

But instead of the storybook detective she'd envisioned, Mike Parker was more like an older version of one of the Dead

End Kids, lean and sexy in his formfitting jeans and T-shirt, street tough and smart mouthed.

Yet despite his disconcerting appearance and the less-than-successful look of his office, she could not rid herself of the impression that Mike was damned good at his job when he wanted to be. A shrewd intelligence lurked behind those lazy brown eyes, and the set of the man's jaw had a bulldog tenacity about it. Sara had a feeling that he could have easily found Mamie's missing son if he had cared enough to do so.

But even after one brief meeting with the man, Sara could sense that that would always be the trick with the cynical Mr. Parker—to make him care.

It was certainly quite beyond her abilities, she thought ruefully. Maybe she could have persuaded Mike to have taken the case if she had just presented it to him differently, as a simple missing-persons matter, told him nothing about ghosts or auras or psychic impressions.

There was only one problem with that. She was tired of pretending. She'd done it for far too many years, stifling the extraordinary perceptions that made her feel strange and different from everyone else, that frequently got her labeled as crazy, even by her own family.

It was only during the past year that Sara had finally developed the courage to face herself in the mirror and say, "My psychic abilities are as real and natural as the color of my eyes and the shape of my nose. I am *not* crazy."

She certainly didn't need a cynic like Mike Parker to chip away at her newfound confidence. Sara touched one hand to her mouth, still tender from the force of Mike's kiss. Or to cause other disturbances of a less spiritual nature.

"No," Sara resolved, forcing herself up from the chair. Setting her chin to a stubborn angle, she cast one last wistful look at the closed office door. "I will manage just fine without the services of Mr. Michael Parker."

Mike lowered his office blinds and peered between the slats, watching as Sara emerged from the building, her gypsy-colored skirt and golden tumble of curls a splash of color on the gray concrete of the pavement below.

Furtively observing her movements, Mike frowned, still not certain what he was expecting to see—Sara being met by one of those idiots from down at Boom Boom's, to have a laugh over the good one they'd just put over on poor old Mike. Or perhaps someone more sinister from his past, melting out of the shadows to congratulate Sara on a performance well-done, the first phase in some elaborate revenge plot to drive Mike Parker round the bend.

"It'd be a real short trip, doll," Mike muttered, at the same time chiding himself for letting his usual suspicious nature and imagination run away with him. He couldn't make either of those scenarios he'd conjured up fit with the wide-eyed and earnest young woman he'd tossed out of his office.

Sara was doing nothing more sinister than pacing distractedly along the sidewalk, totally unaware of her surroundings, the obscene come-on gestures from the construction workers across the street or the interest she was drawing from a gang of street punks hanging out on the corner.

Mike's office wasn't exactly located at one of the swankier addresses in the city. He caught himself tensing, watching until Sara managed to hail herself a cab and was spirited safely away.

Not, he assured himself gruffly, because he cared in the least what happened to Little Miss Blue Eyes. He just wanted to make sure she was really gone. Mike let the blind fall back into place and turned away from the window with a dismissive shake of his head.

Now that he'd had a chance to calm down, he was pretty convinced that Sara had been acting all on her own, that she was nothing more than she seemed, a harmless kook, an angel with her halo screwed on a little too tight.

But she really had you going for a minute there, didn't she, Parker? a voice inside him taunted. *In more ways than one.*

"The hell she did," Mike growled, seeking to deny both the surge of attraction he'd felt for Sara and the fact that she'd managed to shake him. Not even in that one moment when she'd seemed to look straight through him, her blue eyes so clear and honest and searching?

No, not even then. But Mike did admit to an uncomfortable twinge. He had no objection to a woman trying to see through his clothes, but he didn't want anyone probing deeper than that. There were places in the dark, murky backwaters of his mind even he didn't want to go, memories he didn't want dredged out into the light of day.

But Sara Holyfield was no mind reader—not even close. She was about as psychic as…as the wilted plant his secretary had insisted upon leaving on his windowsill to die.

All right, then. So how'd she know about your old wound?

Mike shrugged. A certain knack for perception and a few good hunches. Maybe Sara had even felt the outline of his scar when they had been locked in that clinch. His T-shirt was thin enough. *And how'd she known about the knife?* A lucky guess, that was all.

And as for all that stuff she'd spouted about him being such a miserable and bitter man… The lady was completely off the mark there. Hell, he was doing better now than he had in the two years since he'd quit his job at the police force. Business was good, at least good enough that he could now afford to have a secretary—when Rosa bothered to show up. And his divorce had become final last fall. He was a free man again, free to go out cruising for gorgeous honeys, free to get lucky every night if he wanted to.

Which didn't help to explain why he'd reacted to Sara like a man stranded for years on a desert island, pulling her into his arms and kissing her that way. Or why when Mike tried to dismiss the whole episode, he couldn't seem to get Sara out of his mind.

Settling back into his chair, he reached for the report he'd been working on, but somehow he kept seeing Sara's woebegone face when he shoved her into the outer office and slammed the door closed.

"I came to you because I honestly needed your help, Mr. Parker."

Mike experienced a brief twinge of conscience. He supposed he hadn't needed to get that rough with the poor kid, but she could always find some other investigator. There was bound to be someone who would be happy to play ghost hunt with her and sucker her out of her money.

Another unpleasant thought. Mike thrust it ruthlessly aside. No, he'd done right by getting rid of Sara and forgetting about her.

Because a woman who thought she could read minds and see ghosts, well she was bound to be nothing but trouble. Especially packaged the way Sara was. Her pretty face all vulnerable and innocent, filling a man's head with stupid noble impulses to fight the baser urges her body was arousing in him.

And what a body. Mike stretched back in his chair, latching his hands behind his head. Good thing he'd resolved to stop thinking about Sara. Because if he closed his eyes, he could still remember how tempting her breasts had looked outlined by the sun, how good it had felt to have those soft curves pressed against him. A faint trace of her perfume still lingered in the air and it brought with it the memory of the kiss they shared. He could still feel the sweet surprise of Sara's lips yielding beneath his, the imprint of her body in his arms, warm, fragile and feminine. It was almost as though she had left some—some sort of aura behind.

Aura? Mike straightened abruptly, his eyes flying open wide. Had that thought really come from him? His gaze darted around his office like a man who'd misplaced his mind and was trying to locate it again.

Oh, man! Mike rubbed one hand across his unshaven jaw. If he was starting to entertain thoughts about Sara's aura, he really needed to get out of here for a while, go get himself a cup of coffee or some breakfast. Yeah, likely that was what was wrong with him. He'd gone hungry enough as a kid to know that the world always made more sense on a full stomach.

Shoving an unfinished report in the top drawer, Mike leapt up and strode out of the room. In the outer office, Rosa's modest switchboard was lit up like the neon sign at a strip joint. Mike paused long enough to switch on the answering machine before trudging down three hot airless flights of stairs that connected his office to the outer world.

He emerged into the heat and noisy blare of the street just in time to catch some little blue-haired punk painting graffiti on his office sign.

"Hey," Mike bellowed.

The kid dropped the spray can and took to his heels. Swearing, Mike gave halfhearted chase for half a block, slowed by the heat and the lingering effects of his hangover. As the kid darted down a narrow alley, Mike gave it up in disgust and turned back to see how much damage had been done.

Instead of the usual obscenities, the kid had merely altered the sign to read Ma Parker's Detective Agency, Two Flights Up.

"Great," Mike muttered. Just what he needed—a graffiti artist with a wit. Grabbing some paper napkins that lay tumbled by a nearby trash can, Mike sought to repair the damage before the paint had a chance to dry, but he only succeeded in smearing it worse.

Preoccupied by his cursing and rubbing, he forgot his own cardinal rule about always being aware of what was happening on the street around him. He didn't realize he had company until a finger poked him sharply in the back of his shoulder.

Mike spun around to find himself all but hemmed to the wall by a burly gorilla of a man attired in a chauffeur's uniform, salt-and-pepper hair bushing out from beneath his driver's cap, his coarse ruddy features and slightly crooked nose shoved in Mike's face. It was a nose Mike remembered well. He'd broken it himself. Though he had trouble recollecting the big ape's moniker—Greg or George perhaps—Mike knew all too well the name of the man who held his leash—

Storm. Xavier Storm.

Every muscle in Mike's body went taut, but he masked his tension behind an insolent drawl. "Well, well, if it isn't George of the Jungle. What brings you to this part of town? Isn't the zoo the other way?"

The gorilla's face scrunched up into a mighty scowl beneath

the brim of his driver's cap. "It's *Mr.* George to you, Parker."
He jerked one large callused thumb in the direction of a long
black limo that stood idling at the curbside. "Mr. Storm is
waiting in the car. He'd like to have a word with you."

"I've got one for him." With a dark smile, Mike spat out
the expletive between clenched teeth.

"That's two words," George objected.

"What d'you know? The ape can count." Mike tried to
elbow his way past, but with a low growl the driver clamped
his hand around Mike's upper arm.

Mike shot him a black, warning look, but the goon only
tightened his grip, snarling, "Mr. Storm ain't got no time to
waste with you, wise guy. He told me to request your presence
and I'm requestin'. Now, it can either be at your convenience
or your inconvenience, if you get my drift."

Mike's hand clenched into a fist, his immediate impulse to
deliver a solid blow to the big ape's solar plexus. He didn't
know what stopped him. It was what a younger Mike Parker
would have done. But maybe he was finally starting to get a
little older and wiser. Maybe he remembered too well the result of his last encounter with good old George—three cracked
ribs, a dislocated jaw and a night in jail.

And maybe it was nothing more than the besetting sin that
had landed Mike in a heap of trouble more than once in his
life—curiosity. It had been a couple of years since he had
crossed paths with Xavier Storm and they hadn't exactly
parted on friendly terms. What the hell could Storm possibly
want with him now?

After a brief hesitation, Mike forced himself to relax. "All
right," he said, breaking George's grip with a quick, sharp
movement. "I'll go see your boss. Just keep the paws to yourself. I wouldn't want to have to do anything that would mess
up your pretty uniform."

George gave a contemptuous snort but retreated a step. As
Mike sauntered over to the car, the driver dogged his heels
like a suspicious pit bull preparing to chomp into Mike's ankle
at any moment if he showed any signs of attempting to escape.

Mike noted the limo awaited him, eased next to the yellow

curb of a no-parking zone. But that was typical of Storm's arrogance, Mike thought sourly. From his penthouse high atop his hotel casino at the end of the boardwalk, the man thought he owned the whole damned town.

George stepped forward to open the rear door. He barely gave Mike time to scramble inside the limo before slamming it closed again. Mike sank down into an air-conditioned interior that was better outfitted than his office—dark luxurious leather upholstery, a minibar, a TV, a personal computer and printer. All of it was as sleek, cool and expensive as the man who sat in the opposite corner, speaking into a cellular phone.

Xavier Storm gave Mike a brief nod of greeting and continued with his conversation, which seemed to consist mostly of dictating orders to whoever was on the other end. Storm could have been an ad for *Gentlemen's Quarterly,* not a strand of his thick black hair out of place, his tailored linen trousers crisp, his necktie perfectly arranged, his subtle pinstripe shirt immaculate, the square links that fastened the cuffs simple in design, but obviously solid gold.

He gave an impression of height and power even while lounging in the back of a limo, his hooded green eyes dispassionate, faintly bored as he listened to whatever excuses the subordinate was apparently whining into his ears through the phone. The cast of his features was gaunt, almost predatory. Mike supposed Storm could have been called handsome, if you liked that lean, arrogant look that many women appeared to, including Mike's own ex-wife.

The chauffeur resettled his large bulk behind the wheel of the car. Never missing a beat in his phone conversation, Storm depressed a button, raising a tinted glass, turning the back seat of the limo into a very private, sealed-off world.

"How cozy," Mike muttered, his fingers drumming out an impatient tattoo on the armrest. Between the minibar and a seat large enough to be a bed, Storm really had it made. Make-out city if the rumors about Storm were true. An unwelcome image surged into Mike's head no matter how hard he tried to fight it.

So was it here in the back seat that Storm had seduced Darcy, or had he deemed her worth the cost of a hotel room?

The thought no longer had the power to burn Mike with a jealous rage, but the cold ashes of his hate for Storm remained.

Even if it hadn't been for the bad blood between them over Darcy, Mike feared his dislike of Storm would have still been intense. There was just something about the man and his mocking arrogance that brought out in Mike a side of himself he didn't like. Storm's wealth and breeding was like a slap in the face, a constant reminder to Mike of who he was and where he came from. The son of a no-account gambler and petty con man from the wrong side of the tracks. Little Mikey Parker, the throwaway kid, worth more dead than alive even at the tender age of twelve.

Mike felt familiar bitterness churn through his gut and mumbled, "The hell with this." He reached for the door only to discover it was locked and there was no sign of a release button. Storm chose that moment to end his conversation. Snapping the phone shut and tossing it on top of the minibar, he turned toward Mike with an urbane smile.

"So sorry to have kept you waiting, Mr. Parker," he said in a low purring voice. "It was good of you to agree to meet with me on such short notice."

Mike shot him a glare. "It's not as though I had a helluva lot of choice."

Storm hunched one shoulder in a dismissive shrug. "Mr. George is a very devoted employee. But you have my apologies if he was a little…overzealous in carrying out my commands. I trust I didn't drag you away from anything too important." Storm arched one thin black brow as his gaze roved over Mike's disheveled appearance. "May I offer you anything? A drink perhaps? Or a comb and razor?"

"No thanks, Storm. If I wanted to slit your throat, I would've brought my own."

A glimmer of amusement appeared in Storm's hooded green eyes. "Do I still detect a note of hostility, Mr. Parker? After all this time, I would have thought the little misunderstanding between us long forgotten." After a brief hesitation, Storm asked, "How is Dulcie?"

Mike's jaw clenched. The son of a bitch didn't even remember her name. "*Darcy* is doing just fine for all I know. She's probably living quite well down there in Florida with all the money she managed to clean out of me after the divorce."

"Pity you didn't think to have a prenuptial agreement," Storm drawled. "You could have hardly expected to have formed a permanent relationship with a woman you found in a cake."

"And you'd know all about permanent relationships, wouldn't you, Storm?" Mike said with a sneer. "Didn't I just see in the papers that you finished up your third divorce? In most ball games I've ever heard of, three strikes and you're out."

For a moment, Storm's imperturbable mask slipped and his mouth tightened with what might have been pain if he'd been anything other than the coldhearted man he was. "Perhaps it would be better if I come right to the point."

"Oh? You've got a reason for wasting my time? I'm dying to hear it."

Storm ignored the sarcasm and went on. "I have reason to believe that you may soon be receiving a visit from a woman seeking the services of a detective. A woman from Aurora Falls named Sara—Sara—" Storm frowned slightly as he groped for the name.

Mike gaped at him. He didn't know quite what he'd been expecting this little tête à tête to be about, but it certainly wasn't this. He was so stunned, he forgot his usual caution about volunteering information and supplied, "Holyfield. Sara Holyfield."

Storm's eyes narrowed. "So the young lady has already been to see you." It was more of a statement than a question, but Mike was hardly paying attention.

He still couldn't fathom the connection. Sara and Storm? It was like trying to imagine an angel chatting with the devil over a friendly cup of tea.

"*You* know Sara Holyfield?" he demanded in utter disbelief.

Storm merely raised his brows. "Let's just say I know *of* her."

"You surprise me, Storm. I thought hardheaded businessmen like you confined your money dealings to this world. What've you been trying to do, find a way to take it with you?"

When Storm's brow furrowed in confusion, Mike took a keen pleasure in needling him. "Looks like your sources are holding out on you. Didn't they tell you? Sara's a self-professed psychic. Some kind of a medium." Mike dropped his voice to an exaggerated spooky hush. "The lady deals in ghosts, Storm."

For a moment Storm looked taken aback, then irritated. "That particular aspect of Miss Holyfield's life doesn't interest me. It's her reason for calling upon you that concerns me. She came to ask you to take on a missing-persons case, didn't she? To search for a man named...John Patrick."

"What if she did? What's it to you?"

"Simply this." Storm's reply was soft and chilling. "I don't want him found."

Mike stared at him, astonished. As though he feared he had been too brusque, Storm hurried on. "I don't know what induced this Miss Holyfield to meddle in this affair, but I assure you she has gotten in over her head."

So she had, if Sara was inadvertently doing something to trample on the mighty Storm's toes. Oh, angel, what have you stumbled into here? Mike wondered. Though he maintained his nonchalant pose, all his detecting instincts went on full alert.

"If you know something that would be to my client's benefit, I think you'd better tell me, Storm," Mike said, shoving to the back of his mind the fact that he had thrown Sara out of his office and told her to go get herself a good shrink.

"All your client needs to know is that her quest to find John Patrick should be dropped. You should advise her to do so, and if she refuses to listen, you'd do well to back off from this case yourself, Mr. Parker.''

"Is that some kind of a threat, Storm?"

"Consider it an offer. I would be prepared to triple your usual rates if you could persuade Miss Holyfield to abandon this foolish search."

"And what makes you think you can buy me like a cheap suit?"

Storm's insolent green eyes raked over Mike, from his scuffed sneakers to his T-shirt. "Because, my dear Mr. Parker, I could probably calculate your entire net worth to the nearest penny. And I fear the sum *would* likely be in pennies."

Mike had been told that he was worth nothing in far more blunt ways but none had ever stung worse than Storm's elegant way of expressing it.

He told Storm what to do with himself in a short but pithy terms and reached for the door handle, only to curse in frustration. He'd forgotten he was virtually a prisoner in Storm's little luxury-bound den on wheels.

"I'm sorry if my lack of tact offends you, Mr. Parker. Despite your dislike of me, I bear you no ill will," Storm said, adopting a more conciliatory tone. "I admire your talents and feel they are completely wasted trying to run some two-bit detective agency. I told you that years ago when I first tried to hire you to run security for my casino."

"Well, maybe you should have spent more time trying to tempt me and less time tempting my wife," Mike snarled. "I wasn't interested in working for you then, Storm. And I'm not now. So I suggest you unlock this damned door before I find my own way out of here, like smashing that fancy little computer of yours through one of the windows."

His angry gaze collided with Storm's and held for a moment. Then Storm's heavy lids drifted down, veiling his eyes. Reaching to his side, he depressed a button and the door lock clicked open.

Mike shoved the door open and thrust himself out of the car, but before he even had time to straighten, Storm's silky voice echoed from the cavernous recesses of the limo.

"Parker, one last word of caution. You'd be wise to forget about taking on this case."

"I've never been noted for my wisdom. Have a nice day, Mr. Storm." Mike slammed the door closed and stalked off down the sidewalk without looking back. He charged upstream through a pack of stupid tourists who didn't seem to know that if they wanted to find the boardwalk, they had to head toward the ocean, not away from it.

Crossing against the light, Mike was nearly grazed by a honking taxi and its cursing driver, but he continued blindly on for several more blocks before he managed to cool down.

When he finally paused to draw breath, he was more irritated with himself than Storm. Irritated that even after all this time, he'd still let the guy get to him.

"What a morning," he muttered. First the queen of the gypsies and now the casino king, the two of them bizarrely connected by a ghost and a missing chump named John Patrick. It was like stumbling into the plot of an old mystery movie after you'd missed the whole first reel.

But it wasn't his mystery, Mike reminded himself. Then why had he allowed Storm to believe he'd taken on Sara as a client? The answer was simple. For the first time since he'd met the guy, the smooth-polished Mr. Storm had actually seemed capable of breaking into a sweat like any ordinary Joe. Whether he was alive or dead, this John Patrick person obviously posed some sort of threat to Storm, which meant he had something to hide—a fact that didn't surprise Mike at all.

Nobody pulled down the kind of millions and deals that Storm had and did it completely honestly. That was a bitter truth Mike had learned long ago from watching the antics of his own father. The only difference between Storm and Mike's old man, was that Storm appeared to be the better gambler.

But maybe his luck was about to run out. Mike's mouth set into a grim line. He'd owed Storm one for a very long time, and not just because of that business with Darcy. Even more because Mike had an innate dislike of all cheats and con men. And behind that Ivy League manner and prominent Philadelphia family background, Mike had always had a gut feeling that Xavier Storm would prove to be the biggest fraud of all.

The more he thought about it, the more nosing around into this Patrick business began to appeal to Mike.

Are you sure that's what's appealing to you? his inner voice tormented. *Or the excuse to see a certain big-eyed, curly-haired angel of a blonde again?*

"No way!" Mike blurted out so loud that he startled several teenagers passing by. But despite his denial, he was once again overpowered by that feeling of Sara melting in his arms.

He was quick to shut it down with a vehement shake of his head. Despite the sizzling kiss they'd shared, he didn't want to be anywhere near a woman who read tea leaves, who might want to try reading him. If he decided to go looking for John Patrick, he'd do it on his own, Mike resolved. "I can do just fine without the psychic services of Miss Sara Holyfield."

Long after Mike Parker had slammed his way out of the back seat, the black limo continued to idle at the curbside. His shoulders slumped, Xavier Storm leaned forward, bracing his head upon his hands in a display of weariness he never allowed anyone else to see.

Waiting for some instructions from his employer, Storm's driver eventually became concerned and lowered the tinted glass himself. Twisting around in his seat, Mr. George glanced anxiously back at Storm. "You okay, boss? You get that business with Parker all taken care of?"

With a long sigh, Storm straightened. "No, I handled the situation rather badly. I fear I overplayed my hand, Mr. George."

A mistake Xavier Storm rarely made, but his usual icy calm had been badly shaken ever since he'd stumbled across the advertisement in the papers and realized that someone was looking for John Patrick. Why? After all these years? When he'd recovered from his initial shock, he initiated a few careful inquiries after the person who'd placed the ad, only to discover the situation had already grown worse.

Only yesterday morning, Miss Holyfield had cheerfully informed the newspaper she was discontinuing her ad in favor of a more direct approach. She was off to Atlantic City to hire herself a famous investigator, Mr. Michael Parker.

Storm's mouth twitched into a grim smile that held little humor. "Of all the detectives in New Jersey, why did that foolish girl have to drag Parker into this?" he murmured.

"I dunno, boss." Mr. George's deep-set eyes darkened with concern. "But what are you going to do? If Parker and the Holyfield girl succeed in finding the truth about John Patrick…" the chauffeur trailed off.

"If they succeed, Mr. George?" Storm's face set in taut lines, his voice assuming its customary dangerous purr. "Well, we will simply have to make certain that they don't."

Three

Mike guided his lipstick red Mustang convertible down the shaded streets of Aurora Falls. It was definitely a one-fast-food-joint type of little burg with Yuppie pretensions. Even the quickie mart sported a blasted pink-and-white awning.

As he turned the corner onto a street that looked suspiciously like one he'd already been down, his radio speaker blared out the sound of the Eagles warning him to take it easy. Probably way too loud for Dullsville, so Mike leaned over and switched the cassette tape off.

He brushed aside a bead of sweat trickling down his brow. The afternoon sun baked down through the open top of the convertible, making Mike curse his choice of apparel—dress blue jeans, his best T-shirt topped off with a navy sports jacket. Mike Parker, P.I. in his professional mode. Ready, perhaps, to make a better impression on Miss Sara Holyfield.

No way! Mike scowled his denial, quick and sharp, that his spiffed-up appearance had anything to do with Sara.

Oh, yeah? a voice inside him taunted. And so who's the

close shave, the freshly trimmed hair and the liberal dose of Mr. Manly cologne supposed to be for? The ghost?

Mike was beginning to find his inner voice damned annoying, especially when it was right. Okay, maybe he had given a thought or two to Sara when he'd spent that extra five minutes in front of the mirror this morning. If he wanted the woman's cooperation, he had a few fences to mend with her after the way he'd treated her yesterday. Making a pass at her, flinging out sarcastic insults, chucking her out of his office.

When he saw her again, he'd be lucky if she didn't tell him to go to hell. If he hoped to get any information out of her regarding this Patrick business, then he was going to have to turn on a little charm, a pretty scarce commodity with him.

But first, he was going to have to find her. After Sara had left yesterday, he tossed all the information he'd taken down about her straight into the trash. And wouldn't you know it? It *would* be the one day Rosa would creep into work and decide to make herself useful by tidying up his office. Sara's address and phone number were now buried somewhere in a city Dumpster.

But it shouldn't be too difficult for Mike to locate her in a small town like this, should it? After all, he was supposed to be a detective. Squeaking through on the yellow end of a traffic light, Mike whipped the Mustang onto what he presumed to be Aurora Fall's main street.

Mostly because there was a sign that proclaimed helpfully Main Street. The wide boulevard planted with skinny striplings of trees and lined with a row of spanking new shops, tried desperately to convey an impression of old-moneyed charm. Like a gaggle of ladies wearing bonnets, almost every shop front was adorned with one of those prissy awnings, except for—

Mike slammed on the brakes, staring through his windshield at the store set midway down the block. Instead of an awning, its doorway was overhung by a huge mechanical eye, winking open and closed, the Plasticine lashes drifting coyly up and down. Beneath this device dangled a sign announcing the store's name in bright red letters. The Omniscent Eye. Then in small print, New Age Bookstore.

And Mike had been wondering how difficult it was going to be to find Sara Holyfield. As he studied the sign, a slow grin spread over his face. He didn't realize he was holding up traffic until a horn blared loudly behind him.

"All right, all right," Mike groused.

Easing his car into the nearest parking space, Mike got out, fed some change into the meter and then sauntered down the sidewalk for a closer inspection of Sara's shop front. While the monster eye whirred merrily over his head, Mike couldn't help chuckling to himself. He was able to imagine what a stir Sara's advertising device must be creating with her nearest neighbors, a petite sizes boutique where Mike could see a snooty blonde working behind the counter, and on the other side an antique "emporium" complete with bay window. Mike liked Sara all the better for what must be her defiance of the local awning-and-swirly-sign dress code.

Ducking down, Mike paused to check his reflection in the shop glass, wetting his fingers and slicking down a stray cowlick of hair. Reaching for the handle, he pushed open the door.

As he entered the store, a symphony of chimes tinkled, but the noise was almost lost in the other sounds that swirled around him—wall speakers pouring forth the sounds of pattering rain, birdcalls and chittering monkeys. The illusion of having strayed into some kind of tropical rain forest was helped by the fact that plants littered the surface of counters, fronds and ferns everywhere, green waxy-looking leaves sprouting lush and exotic flowers.

Although small and cramped with merchandise, Sara's shop seemed somehow cool and soothing after the bustle of summer traffic outside. The place smelled of books and some subtle fragrant incense. As the door eased softly shut behind him, Mike caught himself glancing around.

Shelves lined with texts promised to help him with everything, from thinking himself thin to channeling his past lives. Crowding the aisle were displays of tarot cards, herbal remedies, incense stacked like cinnamon sticks in glass jars, meditation tapes and CDs. Mike didn't bother looking closer at those. Somehow he doubted he would find familiar musical groups tucked in among them.

Flicking one finger over a weird-looking goddess incense burner, Mike pulled a wry face. He supposed someone must buy this stuff considering some of the things his old man had been able to palm off on unsuspecting marks.

But thinking about his father was only sure to darken his day and Mike was in a reasonably good mood for once. He didn't want to spoil it, so he was quick to shunt all thoughts of Robert Parker aside.

Edging cautiously past a stand filled with scented candles, he nearly bumped his head against some sort of circular rope hanging adorned with feathers, the sort of thing that could have been woven by a demented spider.

He was beginning to feel a little like the Alice kid who'd jumped down a manhole or something only to find herself alone in some kind of strange wonderland. The shop seemed deserted. But at the back of the store, he saw a doorway hung with a beaded curtain.

He headed for it and found the glass counter display of crystals and silver jewelry. An old-fashioned cash register that would make a satisfying ring when recording a sale sat on the well-polished surface.

Behind the counter, perched on a stool, her head bent over a book, was Sara. She didn't even seem to have noticed that anybody had come into her shop. A customer could waltz in and rob her blind. But perhaps she didn't have that kind of problem in a store like this. Maybe shoplifting spiritual doo-dads was considered bad karma.

Mike paused a moment to study Sara before making his presence known. She was just as beautiful and angelic as he'd remembered. Today she wore her hair pulled up high into a ponytail, ringlets falling down like a silken blond cascade, drawing attention to the delicate nape of her neck. Dark-framed reading glasses balanced on the tip of her nose, magnifying the solemn intensity of her blue eyes, making her look at once sweet and sexy and…

And those were exactly the kind of thoughts that had gotten him into trouble with Sara Holyfield yesterday. Mike reined himself in sharply—he was here for business, strictly business. Find out exactly how much Sara knew about John Patrick and then get the hell out of this voodoo joint.

Mike took a step closer to the counter and cleared his throat.

"Yes? May I help you?" Sara asked, looking reluctantly up from her book with a bright smile. Her gaze collided with his and she froze. Her lovely smile faded and Mike was sorry to see it go. But he supposed he could hardly have expected any different.

"Mr. Parker," she said after a painful pause. "What—what a surprise."

Mike summoned up his most charming smile. "Yeah, I guess it is. I just happened to be passing through Aurora Falls and I noticed the shop and thought what the heck? I might as well look you up."

"Really?" she asked politely, but doubt shadowed her porcelain-fine features. The woman was too nice to come right out and call him a liar, but Mike almost wished she would glare at him, shout, order him out of her store. Anything but barrage him with this sad and watchful silence.

After another of those awkward hesitations, she removed her glasses as though she liked him better out of focus. "After yesterday, I never expected to see you again."

"Well," Mike started to drawl, then stopped. No, breezy and casual clearly wasn't going to work here. Time to revert to an enchantingly frank and sincere apology.

"Actually," he said, straightening a little. "The truth is I wasn't just passing by. I came here on purpose to find you. Ever since you left my office, I kept thinking that I'd been a little abrupt with you."

"A little?" Sara's lashes drifted down as she toyed with the binding of her book. "You accused me of being a charlatan and a lunatic. You slammed your office door in my face."

Her words were very matter of fact, but beneath the calm,

he caught the barest threading of hurt. He'd far rather she be ready to smash her crystal ball over his head.

She sat there with that quietly wistful expression, that sad, sad look in her eyes, until Mike squirmed, feeling like the kind of creep that goes around kicking helpless kittens and telling kids there isn't a Santa Claus.

Dropping all pretense and slick moves, Mike stepped straight up to the counter and heaved a gusty sigh. "Look, Sara, I—I'm really sorry. I know I behaved like a total jerk. I guess I was—um—having a bad aura day. But give me another chance, okay?"

He bent down to peer coaxingly into her face. "My aura's much better today. Wanna feel?"

"No, thank you," she said. Her lips twitched with the beginnings of a smile, although she whipped her hands off the counter and safely out of his reach.

She risked a look up at him and he saw that the light was back in her eyes. They stared at each other for a long moment, and to Mike it seemed as though the air in the shop suddenly changed, becoming closer, warmer, heavier with the weight of something. Auras, incense. Hell, he didn't know what it was. He just found himself leaning closer, pulled in by the tug of her big blue eyes, overcome by the urge to kiss Sara full on the mouth.

Their lips were little more than a whisper apart when Sara blinked and took flight, scrambling off her stool like a startled butterfly. Taking a wary step back, she folded her hands, saying, "Well, it—it was very nice of you stop by."

Mike jerked upright, wondering once again what the hell had come over him. Sara's tone sounded nervous, but dismissive. He'd better get his act together and remember what he'd come here for. Time to lay all his cards on the table.

"Actually," he confessed, "I didn't come all the way to Aurora Falls just to apologize."

"Oh? Then why are you here, Mr. Parker?"

"Not Mr. Parker," he said with a trace of irritation. "I asked you to use my first name, remember?"

"Alright...Michael."

Michael? Alarm bells should have been going off in his head. But somehow he liked the way she said it, as light and silvery as the little chimes that tinkled over her doorway. Then, too, he was distracted as she came out from behind the counter.

Flowed out would have been a more accurate description. She had to be one of the most graceful women he'd ever known, and he considered himself an expert on the wiggle and jiggle of the feminine form. His ex, Darcy, had moved with a blatantly sultry sway, very earthy, but Sara seemed to float on a cloud, enticing a man with thoughts of more heavenly pleasures.

A sundress of shimmering blue swirled to midcalf about her shapely legs, the silky pattern bespangled with little stars and half-moons as though Sara had draped her willowy form in a bit of heaven. The bodice was modest and sweet rather than plunging, but the effect was somehow even more tantalizing, thin spaghetti straps keeping the fabric tugged well up and over the gentle swell of her breasts.

Was she wearing a bra today? Mike caught himself wishing for a blaze of sunlight when the sound of Sara's voice called his wayward male mind back to order.

"Michael?" she said in a tone that suggested she'd been forced to repeat herself. "Just why are you here, then?"

Why was he here? Mike wrenched his eyes from the curve of Sara's breast. Why was he here? Oh, yeah.

He paced off a few steps, jingling the change in his pockets if for no other reason than to make sure he kept his hands to himself. "It just so happens," he said, "that I unexpectedly cleared up some of the things I'd been working on, so now I have a little time available. I've reconsidered the case you brought me and decided I can take it after all."

"Oh," Sara said softly.

Oh? That was it. Just *oh?* Mike felt unreasonably piqued. He hadn't expected her to fling herself at him in a fit of gratitude, but it wouldn't have hurt her to show some enthusiasm. Maybe she hadn't understood him, so he added, "What I mean is that I can help you find your missing dude. John Patrick, wasn't it?''

Sara nodded, showing she understood quite clearly. Then she floored him by demanding, ''Why?''

''Why? Why, what?''

''Why did you change your mind so suddenly?''

Mike stifled a grimace. He should have guessed she might ask that, but he was not prepared to tell her that he was out to nail Xavier Storm. That he thought John Patrick might be the key. Somehow Mike couldn't picture his angel going in for revenge as a good motive, so he hedged, saying, ''I told you, I've got some time to kill and your case sounded…um, interesting. And I can use the extra work. That's all there is to it.''

''Is it?'' She gave him one of those looks he didn't like, soft and clear and searching. He didn't know if there was really anything to this psychic business, but he did his best to block his thoughts until Sara averted her gaze.

''Yes, those are my reasons,'' he insisted. ''Now if you've got the time to fill me in on some stuff, I'd like to get started today.''

Sara didn't reply immediately. A tiny furrow marred her brow and then she said, ''I'm very sorry, Michael. But I'm afraid you've driven a long way for nothing. I don't need your services any longer.''

''Why? Have you already hired another detective?'' Mike was surprised to feel a stab of jealousy tear through him.

But to his relief, Sara shook her head. ''No, I've simply decided that I can handle finding John Patrick on my own. I checked this book out of our local library yesterday evening.''

''Book? What kind of book?''

Sara turned back to the counter and reluctantly produced for his inspection the book she'd been reading.

''*You Too can Be a Detective: Find Anyone in ten Days or Less*. By John L. Geyser.'' Mike read the title aloud and snorted with contempt. ''Oh, yeah, and I'll bet it took this Geezer almost a whole week to write this thing.''

Sara whisked the book out of his sight. "I might have known you'd make fun of it."

"Hey, no, I think it's great. I wish you'd show me where this library is and maybe I can find me a book. *How To become a Psychic Overnight.*"

"Don't be ridiculous," she said with a trace of annoyance in her voice. "Of course, everyone does have some psychic ability, but it can take years to develop, that is unless you have a strong natural aptitude for it."

"Kind of like the ability to be a good detective, hmm?" Mike drawled.

She sighed. "Point taken, but that doesn't change anything. I still don't think I should hire you."

"Why not? You sure were convinced yesterday that I was the man for the job."

"But that was before..."

When she hesitated, Mike supplied flatly, "Before you'd been exposed to the full force of my charming personality."

"I don't want to hurt your feelings, Michael," she continued solemnly. "But you do have a very disturbing aura. You're such a cynical man and I'm afraid I've dealt with too much cynicism. Even when I was a little girl, I remember the whispers. *"There goes Sara Holyfield, the goofy kid who thinks she has ESP, the nut who imagines that she can talk to ghosts,"* she mimicked bitterly. "And those were the people who were being kind. You can't even imagine some of the other remarks."

Oh, yes, Mike could. All too well. The world was full of wise asses, just like himself. He recalled some of the quips he'd tossed at Sara. And here she was, worried about hurting his feelings.

Squirming a little, he rubbed the line of his jaw. "Look, Sara, about some of those things I said to you yesterday. I didn't mean anything personal. It's just...you're right. I am a cynic. I don't believe in much of anything, not even myself. Hell, I've always been that way. Even as a kid.

"When my foster mom dragged me off to see *Peter Pan*, there was this part where everyone was supposed to clap to save that fairy, Stinker Bell or whatever her name was. Well, if it had been up to me, I'm afraid the little sprite would have died.''

Sara laughed, but she gave him one of those looks he was both coming to like and dread, brimful of sympathy and understanding, as though she were seeing things about him he didn't even see himself.

''That, I fear, is the great difference between us, Michael,'' she said. ''I've struggled for a very long time to keep my fairies alive. So while I do appreciate your offer to take my case, I think it would probably be better for both of us if I declined. But thank you, anyway, for stopping by.''

Her rejection was sweet but firm, and Mike should have let it go at that. Hell, she was right. He didn't believe in any of her psychic or supernatural nonsense and he never would. Even without her cooperation, he could dredge up enough information himself to find this Patrick guy and make him a permanent thorn in Storm's multimillion-dollar behind.

But Sara's refusal to work with him bugged Mike on a level he couldn't explain. He caught himself trailing after her around the shop while she watered her plants.

''Listen,'' he said, ''what if I was able to keep my negative vibes to myself?''

Sara cast him a doubtful glance.

''No, really, you said yourself you didn't need me to handle the—er—ghost hunting part of this case, just to conduct the search for John Patrick. So you take care of the more... spiritual things and I'll deal with the nitty-gritty realities. It'd be the perfect marriage.'' Mike winced as though he'd said a dirty word. ''The perfect partnership, I mean.''

Sara hesitated, her watering can suspended over the next fern. Mike rushed on to press his advantage. ''We wouldn't even have to work that closely. I could give you my reports over the phone.''

She fretted her lower lip, then conceded, ''That might work.''

''And you really don't honestly think you can track down Patrick yourself, using that book, do you?''

"N-o-oo," Sara answered slowly, setting down her watering can. She was weakening. She was definitely weakening. But Mike was careful not to let any signs of triumph escape him. Like a good hunter, a skilled detective knew how not to spook his quarry.

"I'd have to know what your rates are," Sara said.

"Oh, we don't need to worry about those just now."

"Yes, we do. We never got around to discussing it yesterday, but I have to be certain I can afford you."

Mike started to sidestep the question, then shrugged. What the hell difference did it make? She was never going to see a bill from him anyway.

"Um…" He paused, then rattled off the lowest possible figure he thought she'd believe. "I work for ten dollars a day, plus expenses."

"Ten dollars a day?" Sara's eyes widened. "That's very reasonable."

"I'm a very reasonable fellow. So do we have a deal?"

"I suppose we'll have to draw up some kind of contract?" she asked.

"Nah, I'm not much of a guy for paperwork. A simple verbal agreement will do. And a handshake."

He extended his palm toward her. After another brief hesitation, she slipped her small slender hand into his grasp. He felt a burst of strange, warm and wonderful feeling, as though he'd suddenly been doused in sunshine. And then a jolt of pure panic.

What the hell was he doing? This was still the same sweet, slightly scatty gypsy lady he'd run off yesterday. And yet, here he stood, pumping her hand and grinning like an idiot who'd just won first prize in the lottery.

It was a soft, silky hand that he didn't seem to be in any hurry to let go of. Her fingers curled around his, striking off those unexpected sparks of desire he'd experienced yesterday, along with sensations that were far more alarming. Like the urge to look deep into those big blue eyes of hers and raise that delicate hand of hers to his lips.

Dropping Sara's hand as though he'd suddenly seized hold

of the smoking hot barrel of a pistol, Mike retreated a wary step. He tried to reassure himself that he hadn't just gone off his rocker. He had a good reason for striking up this bargain with Sara. It was the best way to gain her confidence and to get what he wanted from her. Using her to get the goods on Storm was his only interest in little Miss Blue Eyes.

Sure it is, Parker and every chump that wanders into Storm's casino comes away a winner, Mike's inner voice scoffed.

But Mike ignored it.

"So, okay," he said briskly, rubbing his hands together. "I'd like to get started on the case right away, Sara. Do you have any facts that I can use to begin tracing Patrick? Cold hard facts, evidence, not any crystal ball stuff."

"Well, there are some old photographs and things in a jewel box out at the old Pine Top Inn."

"Good, let's go get them."

"All right." Sara nodded, but an uneasy expression crossed her face. "Michael, I know you don't want to be involved with the more spiritual side of this case. But if you want to take any information away from the Pine Top Inn, there is someone's approval you're going to have to get."

"Who's that?"

"Mamie."

"No problem. I'm sure I can get around any dame—" Mike froze, his jaw dropping as he suddenly remembered who Sara was talking about.

Mamie Patrick.

The ghost.

Four

Mike's red Mustang sped past the outskirts of Aurora Falls, heading down the winding road that led toward Old Pine Lake. The rush of wind through the open top of the convertible tugged strands of Sara's hair loose from her ponytail and left her feeling slightly breathless.

Or perhaps that last phenomenon could be more accurately attributed to the man seated behind the wheel, his determined male aura capable of filling the interior of this tiny car and then some.

There'd been a brief moment when Sara had thought she'd lost him, as soon as the subject of Mamie's ghost had come up again. But whatever smart-aleck remark had hovered on the tip of his tongue, for once, Mike had been able to swallow it.

He'd hardly waited long enough for her shop assistant to return from lunch before whisking Sara out the door and into his car.

As the Mustang raced down the road, the roar of the wind in their ears made conversation difficult and Sara was glad of it. She needed time to think. Unlike Mike, she wasn't used to rushing into anything. Before she had ever decided to visit his detective agency, she'd spent a whole afternoon meditating over the rightness of her choice. And last night, she'd convinced herself that she really was not disappointed she'd been unable to hire Mike, that she was better off without ever seeing him again.

That was why it had been very disconcerting to have him pop up in her shop today, like a genie uncorked from a bottle. And if genies looked the way he did, no woman would bother rubbing the lamp again to wish for anything more.

Sara's eyes strayed to where Mike's tall frame lounged behind the wheel, his attention focused on the road ahead. They were cramped so close together, she couldn't help being aware of the lean, hard muscle encased in the tight legs of his jeans, the broad reach of shoulders that made him seem all solid male. The rumpled lion of yesterday was gone, his tawny hair obviously freshly trimmed, his rock-hard jaw clean shaven. It should have made him look tamer, but somehow it didn't.

Noticing such things was a new and disturbing sensation for Sara. The man exuded enough sensuality to tempt a nun to set aside her veil, and for some reason, Sara found the tune of an old country tune running through her head. Something about the devil and never realizing he'd have blue eyes and blue jeans.

But Mike's eyes were a very wicked brown. Sara wished she knew what was going on behind them, but he'd shielded himself behind a pair of dark sunglasses. It made her a little uneasy. It wasn't her nature to be suspicious, but she wasn't certain she completely trusted Mike Parker.

A part of her was glad, even grateful he'd decided to take on her case after all. As much as she pretended, she hadn't been fully confident about her ability to find John Patrick on her own. It would be a relief to leave that up to Mike, and yet...

She would have felt better if she knew the real reason behind his sudden change of heart. He was holding something back. She had been able to sense it from the moment he appeared in her shop. But for a man who placed no faith in mind readers, Mike was doing a damned fine job screening his thoughts.

As though becoming aware of her intense regard, Mike angled his head slightly in her direction and smiled. "I don't mind you sitting there admiring my manly profile, angel, but I hope you're paying some attention to the road, because I don't have a clue where we're going."

"You're doing okay," Sara called back above the wind. "Just keep heading straight. In another mile or so, fork to the right past the lake and then we'll be there."

"Do you think Miss Mamie will be at home to callers this afternoon?"

"It's not as though she has anywhere else to go, Michael," Sara replied dryly.

Mike's smile widened into a grin. He was humoring her about her belief in the ghost. Sara realized it, but his teasing had a more gentle edge to it than yesterday.

All the same, she couldn't help wondering what was going to happen when Mike Parker, skeptic extraordinaire, crossed the threshold into Mamie Patrick's domain. Sara had to admit she was anticipating the encounter with something approaching an unholy glee.

The fork in the road appeared and Mike steered toward the right, smooth macadam giving way to gravel. When a spray of pebbles chunked off the side of the Mustang, he swore under his breath and slowed the car down.

A forest of straggly pines closed in about them. Between the dark, weathered trunks, Sara caught glimpses of shimmering blue-green water. On the far side of the lake, echoed the laughter and squeals of summer day camp children swimming on the west shore.

But on this side all was shadows and silence. Even the calls of the bobolinks and chittering squirrels seemed more subdued here.

Mike eased the car almost to a crawl as the road narrowed to little more than a dirt track with a tall sign post pointing the way. A wooden placard hung from the rusted pole, looking like something that should be perpetually creaking in the wind or illuminated by jagged flashes of lightning. Ye Old Pine Top Inn, it proclaimed in well-worn letters.

It was the perfect herald for the deserted building set back amongst the stand of pines. The old clapboard inn was a large, rambling structure with as many turrets and towers as a medieval fortress. Paint cracked and peeling, shutters hanging askew, the broad veranda appeared neglected and unwelcoming.

Braking the car to a halt in front of the porch steps, Mike shut off the ignition. He peeked over the rims of his glasses at the inn and let out a long low whistle.

"So this is it, huh? Ye Old Pine Top Inn. I'll have to put it on my list of favorite overnight stops, right up there with the Bates Motel."

"The present owner, the Jorgensen Realty Co., is trying to fix the place up a bit," Sara said. "They're hoping to restore it into one of those quaint little out-of-the-way places that would attract the better class of tourist trade."

"Sounds a little like trying to turn Dracula's castle into a cozy bed and breakfast. But what the hey." Mike shrugged. "It's not my money."

He made no move to get out of the car, fishing out a pen and small notebook from his inner breast pocket instead. "You probably better tell me where to find this Jorgensen. I might need to talk to—"

"No!" Sara blurted out in alarm. When Mike glanced toward her, clearly surprised, she struggled to speak more calmly, "I—I mean, no, that won't be necessary. They would be of no help at all. They haven't owned the inn long. Mamie lived here way before their time, when the inn was more of an old boardinghouse. The Jorgensens don't know anything. Nothing at all."

She must have still sounded too vehement because Mike removed his sunglasses and continued to stare at her.

Sara realized she'd never hold up well under an intense police grilling. Mike didn't even have to question her. One long silent stare and she was ready to spill her guts.

Pleating her hands nervously in the folds of her dress, Sara sighed and confessed, "All right. Mrs. Jorgensen doesn't even know that I've been coming out here to communicate with Mamie. We're not on the best of terms. Me and Ralph and Elaine Jorgensen, that is. Their development company has been one of the prime movers behind the program to refurbish Aurora Falls, turn it into something a little more upmarket. And—and—"

"They don't exactly appreciate the ambience of your little shop?" Mike filled in when Sara floundered.

Sara nodded unhappily. "I would have never dreamed of coming near their inn under normal circumstances. But I kept hearing the rumors about it being haunted and I just couldn't resist stopping by for a peek. Then I discovered Mamie and—well, you know the rest."

"So in other words, we're trespassing," Mike said flatly.

"Yes."

"I wish you'd told me sooner."

"I'm sorry. I should have warned you that what we are doing is illegal. I wouldn't blame you if you wanted to turn around and go back."

To her chagrin, Mike seemed prepared to do just that. Without another word, he tossed his sunglasses on the dash and turned on the motor. A look of deep concentration on his face, he put the car in gear. But not in Reverse.

He guided the Mustang carefully along the rutted drive, around the side of the inn, easing the car deep within a stand of pines as gently as a mother tucking her baby in bed.

"There," he said, switching off the ignition again. "Not exactly hidden. But at least the car won't be sitting out front like a flaming red flag."

When he realized she was staring at him in astonishment, a deep bark of laughter rumbled from his chest.

"Honey, you really couldn't have imagined I'd go off into a dither at the thought of doing something a teeny bit illegal, did you? I played hookey from the time I was in grade school. The one sure way of getting me to class would have been to tell me it was off-limits."

Sara felt her cheeks flame with an embarrassment as red as Mike's car. Of course. She might have known he'd be the sort of man used to taking risks and bending the rules. He'd probably done far worse and more dangerous things in his life than mere trespassing. But she still felt daring and guilty over the time she sneaked a cigarette in junior high.

"You must find me incredibly naive," she said in disgruntled accents.

"No, merely adorable."

He still looked amused, but the light in his eyes was tender as he bent down and brushed his lips against hers. It was a chaste kiss, quick and almost brotherly. But it was enough to remind her of the far more passionate embrace they'd shared yesterday and leave her feeling completely flustered.

She still hadn't fully recovered by the time Mike eased himself out of the car and came around to open her door.

"Take it easy," she told her madly thumping heart. It was just a friendly gesture and meant nothing. Mike obviously went around kissing women right, left and center without a second thought. And most of those women were probably as casual about it as he was. Sometimes Sara thought she was the only female left in this century who regarded kissing as something special, a highly personal and intimate contact.

Mike offered her a hand and Sara clambered out of the car, somewhat unsteadily, bringing with her a paper trail of envelopes that Mike had left scattered about. A few days' worth of mail, he hadn't had a chance to go through, Mike had explained before blithely shoving the whole stack onto the floor mat.

Now as she straightened, several of the envelopes tumbled to the grass beside the car. She and Mike nearly bumped heads, swooping to retrieve them. While Mike chased down several that had fluttered near the front tire, Sara went after the one that had landed at her feet.

It was a business-size envelope, thickly padded as though it contained several pages worth of letter. As soon as her fingers closed around it, an odd feeling swept through Sara, as disturbing and powerful as though some sort of dark mist seeped from beneath the seal of the envelope.

She had discovered long ago that she had limited psychosometric powers. Not as strong as some psychics she'd read about but enough to sometimes divine details about the owner of an item or to guess the contents of package. It was an ability that had frequently gotten her into trouble as a child, left her open to accusations of having peeked at Christmas presents early.

But this letter was no Christmas present. It was something black and empty. It felt heavy in her hands, almost threatening. The return address was a little smudged, but still partly readable. *Trenton State...* Sara became aware of Mike beside her, tossing the envelopes he had chased down back into the car.

"Nothing but bills," he said with a cheerful grimace. "I should have just let them blow away. What have you got there—" he began, then broke off as he focused in on the envelope she held. He tensed as though he'd taken a fist to the gut and then snatched the letter from her. She felt strangely relieved to have it out of her hand.

"I—I'm sorry," she faltered. "I didn't mean to pry into your mail. I just picked it up and then—"

"Don't sweat it, sugar. It's nothing important," Mike said, but the edge in his voice told her otherwise. His mouth set in a hard line, an odd look stealing into his eyes. If it had been any other man, Sara would have thought it was fear.

And suddenly, inexplicably, she felt afraid for him.

"It—it's not any kind of bad news, I hope?" she asked.

"Nah," he said tersely. "Just a little fan mail from Trenton State."

"The university?"

"No, the prison."

"Oh." Sara flinched.

Noticing her reaction, Mike angled a sarcastic glance in her direction. "Beg your pardon. I guess *prison* is too blunt for most people these days. *The correctional facility.* Bet you've never known anyone who's had to be *corrected,* have you, angel?"

"My uncle Louie once spent a night in jail for shooting a pellet gun at the neighbor's cat. But he was always quarreling with somebody. Sometimes he could be a—a very unpleasant man and—and..." Sara trailed off, fearing she was sounding hopelessly naive again.

"Yeah, well, my life has been full of people who weren't *pleasant.*" Something bleak and bitter surfaced in Mike's eyes.

Sara's fingers still tingled from her brief contact with the letter. She stared at the envelope with growing uneasiness. Even though she feared Mike would resent the intrusion, she couldn't help asking, "This—this person in prison. He's not writing to threaten you, is he?"

"You mean something like 'I'll get you, when I get out, Lefty.' Good thing my name's not Lefty, isn't it?" A ghost of a smile touched Mike's lips.

When Sara was unable to return the expression, he chucked her lightly under the chin. "Thanks for the concern, angel, but this is nothing for you to get all puckered up about unless you want to find yourself kissed again."

Which, Sara sensed, was Mike's playful way of telling her to mind her own business. He tossed the envelope onto the floor of the car. Then he said briskly, "C'mon, we'd better not keep Miss Mamie waiting. After all, you're paying me by the day. Don't want this spook of yours to end up costing you a fortune."

Giving her no chance to reply, he seized her hand and tugged her along after him around the side of the inn. Sara stumbled in her efforts to keep up with his longer stride, her head still full of the letter he seemed to have dismissed.

But the disturbing vibes she'd picked up from the envelope continued to ripple through her like a handful of pebbles tossed into the serene lake waters of her mind. For a few brief seconds there, she felt as though she'd drawn once more too close to the edge of Mike Parker's world. It was a world where a man could get a knife thrust through his shoulder and be grateful it wasn't his heart. A place where Mike clearly didn't want her probing around and she didn't want to go, fearing what she might find.

It was almost a relief to give herself up to the inn's chilling, but far more familiar aura instead.

As she trailed Mike up the veranda steps, Sara sensed a slight drop in temperature that was a sure sign of a supernatural presence. She marveled that Mike didn't feel it, too, but he tramped heedlessly along the porch, peering in windows. "So which one of these do we have to force open to get inside?" he called out to her.

"None of them. We can go through the front door. It's not locked."

"You people are trusting little souls around here, aren't you?" he drawled.

"No. The Jorgensens have tried to install locks on the doors, but Mamie keeps removing them. She has her own way of dealing with unwanted intruders."

"No kidding? Well, if she ever gets tired of this gig, I could get her a job at Boom Boom's. They're looking for a good bouncer."

Although Sara wasn't proof against his teasing grin, it irritated her that he could be cheerfully oblivious to the inn's brooding presence that was already beginning to weigh so heavy upon her own spirit.

Well, just wait until she got him inside.

Ducking past Mike, she approached the front door, the once-elegant tracery of the oval glass insert now begrimed and cracked. Turning the ornate handle, she thrust the door open. It pushed inward with a loud and eerie creak.

"Great special effects," Mike said.

"You haven't seen anything yet," Sara muttered.

"After you." He waved her inside with a mock gallant bow.

"Nervous, Mr. Parker?" she asked.

"Shaking in my shoes, Miss Holyfield," he replied.

Sara thought she would have dressed up in a bed sheet and yelled "Boo" herself if it would have driven that confident smirk off Mike's face. But she was going to have to leave it up to Mamie to do that.

Preceding Mike across the threshold, Sara stepped into the chamber that in its heyday had been the inn's bustling front lobby. The room stood still and silent, from the great chandelier with its dusty glass globes to the front desk with its pigeonholes filled with rusting keys.

Sara picked her way carefully past a drop cloth, overturned ladder and some paint cans abruptly abandoned by the last work crew Mamie had sent fleeing in terror. The temperature seemed to have dropped several more degrees and Sara could feel the full force of the inn's aura beating down upon her.

The oak-paneled walls seemed steeped with voices long since silenced. Given the inn's troubled history, Sara marveled that Mamie was the only ghost to walk these halls. From the first time she'd set eyes on the place, Sara had sensed that the Pine Top Inn had always been a refuge for lost and tormented souls.

Glancing back at Mike, she saw that he had closed the door and was picking his way carefully past the painters' debris, peering curiously about him. Was it her imagination or was his cocksure manner already a bit subdued?

"Can you feel it?" she asked in hushed tones.

"Feel what?"

"The inn's atmosphere. The air is thick with the aura of broken hearts and broken dreams."

"That's dust, honey," Mike said, and promptly sneezed as if to prove his point. "And stale paint fumes."

He bent down to inspect an overturned paint can that had left a dried crust on the inn's battered wood flooring. "What the hell is this? Eggshell cream," he said, reading the paint label. "Yecch! Looks more the color of baby puke."

"Mamie didn't like it, either. When the painters tried to paint over that lovely old oak wainscoting, she started slapping them with their own paintbrushes. The realty company hasn't been able to get another work crew near the place ever since."

"Sounds like your Mamie has a lot better decorating taste than the Jorgensens." Mike straightened, dusting off his hands and giving her a challenging smile. "So when do I get to meet the old gal?"

Sara frowned at him. "I usually can sense Mamie's where-abouts right away when everything is quiet and still."

"Well, go ahead."

Sara folded her hands, took a deep breath and tried to con-centrate. But to her annoyance, she could sense nothing but Mike's overwhelmingly masculine presence.

The word *still* didn't seem to be in the man's vocabulary. He prowled about like a hunting panther, poking into every-thing. Ducking down behind the front desk, he snooped through all the drawers, then proceeded to rattle his way through the pigeonholes.

"Michael," Sara said at last with an exasperated sigh.

"What?" he asked, glancing back at her.

"I can't sense anything with you being so—so twitchy."

"Sorry." But he didn't even pause as he continued his in-spection, yanking open a door, brushing cobwebs aside as he peeked into a broom closet. "Why don't you just call the old girl and see if she answers you?"

He was being facetious of course, but that was what Sara usually did when she visited the inn alone. Feeling a little embarrassed to do so in Mike's cynical presence, nonetheless, she turned her back on him and called out, "Mamie? Mamie, it's Sara. I've come back and I've brought Mr. Parker with me. You know. The detective I told you might be able to find your son."

"Sure, Mamie," Mike added in a loud voice. "Come on out and we'll chew the old ectoplasm."

Sara whipped around and glared at him.

"Hey," Mike protested with a twinkle in his eye, "I was only trying to help."

"You're going to make her mad. She doesn't like ghost jokes."

"A sensitive spook, huh?"

"And when Mamie's temper is really aroused, she has a tendency to throw furniture at people's heads."

"So did my ex-wife."

He'd been married? Sara was momentarily distracted, won-dering if the ex Mrs. Parker was the one responsible for putting that jaded look in his eyes? No, she sensed that Mike's cynical shell had begun forming years ago when—

"Stop it, Sara," she chided herself fiercely. "It's none of your business."

She should be worrying more about what the reckless Mr. Parker was doing right now. Sauntering over to the stairs that angled upward to the shadowy landing above, he called out playfully, "Hey, Mamie, if you want to meet me, you better get down here or I'm going to start painting the wainscoting again."

"Oh, Mike," Sara groaned. "I really wouldn't do that if I were you."

With a wicked grin at her, Mike continued to coax. "C'mon, Mamie. Not all of us have eternity to wait around. I could die of old age and turn into a spook myself while you keep me standing here."

Sara sucked in her breath. The man was asking for it. And he got it. An icy wind swept through the room and the chandelier began to shake violently.

"What th—" Mike exclaimed. The next instant he went stumbling forward toward the stairs. He was thrown to his knees and would have sprawled flat on his face if he hadn't grabbed the newel post to break his fall.

Sara winced, prepared to duck behind the front desk if paint cans and other stray objects started to fly. But the chandelier gave one more ominous rattle, then all was silent.

Clutching the stair post, Mike slowly regained his footing. Swearing fluently under his breath, he bent down, rubbing his right leg. Sara rushed toward him.

"Michael, are you all right?"

"Yeah, sure." He grimaced. "I just banged my knee up against that blasted post and aw—hell, look at this." He gestured with disgust to where a loose nail had torn a perfect vee in his pant's leg. "Those were my best jeans, dammit!"

"I'm sorry," Sara murmured. "I tried to warn you. You're lucky it wasn't worse."

"What wasn't worse?" he said testily. "I tripped over a loose board or something. That's all."

Sara stared at him incredulous. "You didn't notice that chilling blast of air or the chandelier rattling?"

Mike paused to cast an uneasy scowl up at the light fixture and then shrugged. "It's an old house. There's bound to be plenty of creaks and rattles. That chandelier looks loose. No wonder it shakes when there's a cold draft."

"It's almost ninety degrees outside," Sara pointed out.

"So what? You're trying to tell me a ghost just waltzed through here?"

"I'm not trying, I *am* saying it! Didn't you feel her push you?"

"Oh, for the love of—" Mike broke off his muttered exclamation, then continued in a tone of strained patience. "Sara, I had my eyes open the whole time. If anyone or anything had pushed me, I'd have seen them."

"You can't see Mamie."

"Invisible, is she? No bed sheets or chains?"

"Well, not all the time."

"Ohh. You mean sometimes she does wear chains?"

"No!" Sara snapped, feeling her own temper start to fray. "I mean that sometimes you can catch just a glimpse of Mamie in the window or a mirror."

"And that's how you communicate with her? Mirror, mirror, on the wall, show me the biggest spook of all?"

"No!"

"Then how'd you ever find out about the existence of John Patrick? About him being missing and Mamie wanting to find him."

"It's—it's hard to explain," Sara said. Especially to a skeptic like Mike. "I've never been exactly sure how Mamie speaks to me. But I actually hear her voice in my ear."

"Ah. You hear voices." Mike nodded as if to say he wasn't at all surprised. He was giving her that hateful patronizing look she'd been seeing on people's faces ever since she was three years old.

"Never mind," she choked out. "I should have known better than to ever bring you out here."

"Maybe you should have." Mike stopped rubbing his knee

long enough to eye her with sudden suspicion. "What was the big idea, Sara? You didn't lure me to this inn because you were hoping to get me believing all this supernatural junk, did you? Because if that's what this is all about—"

"No, of course it isn't," she denied hotly, but his charge had just enough truth in it to mortify her. She realized that she *had* been hoping to prove to Mike that Mamie did exist. That Sara wasn't just imagining things or worse still, ready for a padded cell.

But why should she care about proving anything to the arrogant Mike Parker? Almost everyone else thought she was crazy. What did it matter if he did, too?

That was just the trouble. On some level, it did matter. It mattered a lot.

Concealing her dismay, she said, "We came out here to get Mamie's old photographs, remember?"

"Then maybe we better just get them." He sneered. "That is unless your ghost lady has decided she doesn't like me and I can't have them."

Sara glared at him. "No, you can have them. For some reason I can't begin to guess, she likes you well enough."

"How the hell do you know that?"

"You're still here, aren't you?" Sara said with acid sweetness. Brushing past him, she stormed up the stairs, not bothering to look back to see if he followed.

Five

Mike watched in frustration as Sara disappeared into the shadows of the upper hall. Then he sank down on the steps, dangling his hands in front of him, his knee still throbbing.

"Great! Just great," he muttered as he massaged it. Not only had he wrecked his knee and torn his pants, but now he had Sara mad at him.

Well, he'd had a juvenile correction officer once who told him he was enough to try the patience of a saint. Or—Mike glanced ruefully up the stairs at the spot where Sara had vanished—or in this case, an angel.

Mike expelled his breath in a gusty sigh. He hadn't meant to torment Sara about her belief in ghosts. It was just this damned old inn, he thought casting an uneasy glance around the silent, brooding walls.

Much as he hated to admit it, the place had been giving him the creeps ever since he'd set foot inside. Oh, not that he bought into this haunted house stuff or anything like that. Not for a minute. Although there had been a fleeting second when his imagination had worked overtime, when he almost had believed he'd felt a pair of icy hands shoving—

Mike was quick to dismiss the notion. It wasn't Mamie Patrick's spirit bugging him, only the ghosts of his own devising. The ones he carried with him all the time.

Truth was, this damned inn gave him a stupid sense of déjà vu, reminding him too much of the shabby, down-at-the-heels joints he'd been dragged to by his old man. Grand Hotels that weren't quite so grand anymore.

"Someday, Mikey," Robert Parker had always boasted. "Someday it'll be nothing but the Hilton and the Claridge Arms for us."

Mike pulled a wry face, wondering if Mamie Patrick had ever promised her kid stuff like that. If so, she hadn't been able to keep her vows any better than Mike's old man.

She was dead.

And Robert Parker's Hilton had turned out to be Trenton State.

Mike's thoughts shifted grimly to the letter lying on the floorboard of his car. Too bad he hadn't checked his mail more carefully and realized the letter was there before Sara ever saw it, before he had a chance to dwell on it himself. He could have pounced on it, ripped it to shreds, tossed it in the garbage like he always did.

But he'd been reluctant to do that in front of Sara. It might have been far too revealing, and he had a disquieting feeling that his gypsy lady had already seen a whole lot more than he wanted her to.

Holding on to the stair rail, Mike forced himself painfully to his feet. All in all, this case was turning out to be less than comfortable. Now, on top of everything else, he had a streak of dust across the sleeve of his jacket.

Mike slapped at it in disgust, beginning to wonder if all this was worth it, just to get at Xavier Storm.

An image of Storm's arrogant mocking face swam before Mike's eyes.

Yeah, it was, Mike decided with a thin smile.

Turning around, he hobbled stiffly up the stairs to go in

search of Sara. He'd have to apologize for being a jerk. *Again*. But that was okay. He was good at it. He'd spent most of his miserable life being sorry....

Reaching the upper landing, Mike was confronted by a formidable row of doors. But it wasn't too difficult to figure out where Sara had gone. The one at the end stood ajar and he could hear her rustling around.

Limping down the corridor, he peered across the threshold. After the time Darcy had bounced a CD player off his head, Mike had learned to be cautious while entering a room that contained an angry woman.

Sara stood by the windows in the small, stuffy bedroom, trying to throw open one of the casements. Her back was to Mike, but he was certain she was aware of him hovering in the doorway. She stiffened and he could almost swear the hairs at the nape of her neck prickled. But she didn't look ready to bash his head in, so Mike risked coming closer.

Skirting around the end of a cannonball-post bed, he said, "Here. Let me get that."

"No, thank you. I can manage."

Brr! The chill in her voice was colder than the draft that had rocked the chandelier. Mike watched her struggle stubbornly with the window for a moment more before thrusting her impatiently aside.

Tensing his muscles, he forced the casement open with one mighty shove. A breeze filtered in from the direction of the distant lake, making the room a little more bearable.

His macho display obviously made no impression on Sara, but she said stiffly, "Thank you."

So that was it. She wasn't the sort of woman to throw digital clocks when she was annoyed. She was just going to beat him to death with rigid politeness.

He'd have preferred the clock. It was strange. He'd endured the worst of Darcy's temper tantrums with sardonic indifference, only taking care to move out of range. But the quiet stony set of Sara's profile really bothered him.

It was like he was already getting too damn used to basking in the sunshine of the woman's smiles. When she started to move away from him, he caught her by the wrist and said, "Aw, c'mon, angel. There's no need for you to get your wings this ruffled."

"I'm not ruffled," Sara stated, pulling her hand free.

"Yeah, you are." Mike dusted one finger across the bridge of her nose. "When you get annoyed, you get this cute little flush across your cheekbones and the tip of your nose."

Sara went cross-eyed, squinting down as though to see if it was true. Then she stopped, scowling at him.

"I didn't mean to be so short with you downstairs," Mike continued. "But you welshed on our bargain, sugar. You promised you wouldn't try to get me involved with this spook stuff."

"And you promised you'd keep your skepticism to yourself."

"So I did, and I'm sorry. I guess sometimes my mouth moves a lot faster than my brain."

He gave her a coaxing smile. "Friends again?"

Sara nodded. "All right. But no more ghost jokes. You promise?"

"Cross my heart and hope to—er—not die."

Her lips quivered and then her angel's smile was back again, making him feel a little giddy and almost absurdly light-hearted. Sara obviously wasn't the type to hold a grudge. Unlike him. He wondered if she'd ever been able to stay mad at anybody for long.

She seemed to have a very generous and forgiving spirit, almost too good to be true. He'd seen a lot of women come and go, mostly go. But he'd never known one quite like her.

Instead of getting down to business as he should have done, he found himself studying her intently. After a brief hesitation, he said, "At the risk of making you mad again, do you mind if I ask you a personal question?"

"That depends on what it is." She was still smiling, but a certain wariness crept into her eyes.

"What's your angle in all this?"

"My angle?"

"Yeah, what are you hoping to get out of all this Patrick

business? Proof that ghosts do exist? That you really are a psychic? Your picture on the cover of *Supernatural Geographic* or something like that?"

Sara laughed, a sound of genuine amusement, a very kissable dimple hovering at the corner of her mouth. "No, Michael," she said. "I'm not out to prove anything. I gave up trying to make anyone believe in me a long time ago."

"Then what is it?" he persisted. "Why are you taking all these risks, poking around in this decrepit old inn, spending your own money, to find the kid of a woman who died before you were born? Someone you never even knew."

"It's no use me attempting to explain, Michael. You'd never understand."

"Try me," he said, although he wondered himself why he was so interested. Maybe it was because she genuinely baffled him. She was like some bright exotic little bird that had fluttered into the gray pavement of his world, and he really wanted to understand her before she flew off again.

Sara gave him a doubtful glance and spread her hands in a helpless gesture. "I honestly don't know, Michael. Something about Mamie Patrick just touched me. I feel a strange sense of kinship with her. Maybe because I'm a bit of a lost soul myself. Maybe because we're both outsiders here in Aurora Falls."

"You? I thought you were born and raised here."

"I moved here a year ago when I inherited my aunt's shop after she died. I explained all that to you yesterday. Don't you remember?"

Unfortunately, Mike didn't.

"Sorry," he said. "Guess my mind was on more..." His gaze drifted to the delectable curve of her breasts. "On—on your fairies. You're not wearing them today."

"No, I'm not." Sara's hand fluttered self-consciously to the delicate gold chain around her neck that disappeared intriguingly inside her bodice.

Mike couldn't restrain his curiosity. Gently nudging her hand aside, he hooked the gold chain with one finger and reeled up the small gemstone at the other end. It looked like a bit of purple-colored crystal cut in the shape of a prism.

Cupping it in his hand, he asked, "What's this?"

"It's an amethyst. It's supposed to relieve stress and promote a sense of inner calm."

"Does it work?"

A gleam of humor shone in Sara's eyes. "It did until you turned up in my shop."

Mike grinned back, but he realized she was only partly kidding. He could sense the beginning of tension in her because he could feel it stealing over him, a heavy awareness of the intimacy of their situation. Alone together in the cramped confines of the bedroom, him standing so close he could breathe in the fresh scent of her golden hair, his hand suspended just above the soft swell of her breast.

Amusement faded and suddenly they were both staring into each other's eyes a heartbeat too long for comfort. Sara spooked first. Tugging her pendant free of his hand, she tucked it safely back inside her sundress and then moved away, putting a safe distance between them.

"Perhaps we'd better look at the photographs now," she said with a trace of nervousness.

"The photographs?" Mike's gaze longingly charted the course her necklace had taken. He gave a sharp jerk, forcing himself to snap out of it. "Oh, yeah. The photographs. Sure. Get them out."

While Sara rummaged around in the depths of a deep walk-in closet, Mike paced back to the window. He tried to suck in a deep breath of fresh air, but there just didn't seem to be enough of it.

Maybe he didn't understand Sara, but he understood himself too well. A beautiful woman plus the proximity of a bed. It was a simple equation and made for an embarrassing but totally male reaction. All his stiffness now wasn't just owing to his bruised knee.

But it wasn't owing to any strange mystic attraction between him and Sara, either. Just a little jolt of lust in the afternoon—

that's all it was. And he could fend it off by keeping his mind fixed more on the case and less on her.

He prowled about the room, trying to make himself look brisk and busy detecting. After all, he hadn't done much of anything impressive so far besides manage to fall up the stairs. Better convince Sara she'd be getting her money's worth.

But there wasn't a whole lot to inspect. The room was dismally small, almost stark in its furnishings, the bed with its mattress stripped bare, a small dresser and mirror, a rickety bookshelf mounted on the wall, its dusty volumes cracked and yellowed with age.

And of course there was the requisite worn carpet and faded wallpaper. All too depressingly familiar. Mike's urge to play detective left him. All he wanted to do was get the damned pictures and get out of here.

Sara emerged at last from the closet, looking flushed, a small black-lacquered jewel box in her hands.

"There aren't many of Mamie's things left after all this time," she said apologetically. "Just this box she kept hidden beneath a loose floorboard in the closet and those books up there that no one ever bothered to move."

She set the jewel box down on the bed, but Mike made no move to take it. He averted his gaze to the books on the shelves, finding it easier somehow than focusing on Sara's shapely form, the bed looming so suggestively between them.

Not that he expected to gain anything from checking out Mamie's books. They were an uninspiring lot. He grimaced as he read some of the titles.

"Plane Geometry, Biology, Senior English. What great bedtime reading. Better than a sleeping pill."

"Mamie was studying to get her G.E.D. right up until she…" Sara let the thought trail off, unspoken.

Mike wasn't interested in Mamie Patrick as much as he was in the mysterious, missing John and his connection to Storm. But he couldn't seem to help asking, "So what happened to her?"

"She was only twenty-four when she discovered she was dying from leukemia," Sara said softly. "She was planning to put John Patrick up for adoption herself, but she couldn't bear to part with him. She kept putting off the decision until...until it was too late. She simply collapsed one day and had to be rushed to the hospital. She never regained consciousness. When her spirit was finally able to drift back here to the inn, John was long gone.''

"The state welfare people probably swooped in on him. Poor kid.'' Mike grimaced. When had been the last time he had seen his own mother? Had he been six or seven?

He wasn't sure. He couldn't recall her face, but other unwelcome images remained. The sound of sirens, an ambulance stretcher, her hand reaching out to him, a soft voice assuring him that everything was going to be all right.

But of course, it hadn't been. Other memories intruded. He never knew where his father had been during this time, probably off trying to fleece old ladies at bingo or something like that. All Mike recalled was himself, huddled alone on the bed in another hotel room, weeping softly into his pillow. As far as he could remember, it was the last time he'd ever cried....

Mike's gaze dropped to the box on the bed and suddenly he wasn't so sure he wanted to open the damn thing, but Sara was waiting expectantly.

He had to remind himself that the box contained someone else's life story, not his. This all had nothing to do with him. Dragging the jewel case closer, he flipped open the lid. During his career both as a police officer and a detective, he had sorted through someone else's private effects many times and he'd trained himself to remain impersonal about it.

But Mamie's small store of treasures were more pathetic than most. A pair of the colorful plastic "pop" beads that had once been the fad among teenage girls, a cheap zirconium ring that could have come from a Cracker Jack box, a few hair ribbons, a pair of blue baby bootees, a child's stick-figure drawing of a boy and a smiling woman, labeled in proud, crooked letters Mom And Me.

Mike shoved those things aside, going straight for a small cache of black-and-white photographs. They were mostly of the boy. John Patrick playing down by the lake, John Patrick clutching a ragged stuffed dog, John Patrick blowing out the candles on his birthday cake.

He'd been a cute kid, a little on the chubby side with laughing dark eyes. It was hard to tell the color of his hair because he had a crew cut, making him look like a little roly-poly sailor. Some shade of light brown, Mike supposed. Not that it mattered. Kids' looks could change a lot as they aged.

Mike saw how much the boy resembled his mother when he came to the last picture. Obviously Mamie and her son. She didn't look to be much more than a kid herself, despite her high heels, pleated skirt and tight-fitting sweater. John Patrick half hid behind his mother, peeking playfully at the camera, but Mamie's bright smile was strained.

"That was taken on John's sixth birthday." Sara's voice came close by his shoulder, startling him. Mike had been concentrating so hard on the pictures, he hadn't realized she'd moved to stand beside him, a soft kind of sadness clouding her eyes.

"That was the last happy day Mamie ever spent with her son," Sara continued. "Even then she realized how sick she was and worried about John Patrick's future."

"And who's the bald old geezer lurking in the background?" Mike pointed to the grizzled old man in coveralls standing just behind Mamie's shoulder.

"That's Mr. Kiefer. He was the groundskeeper and short-order cook. The people that owned the inn used to serve lunches and dinners here besides running the boardinghouse. Mamie helped with the waitressing and cleaning. That's how she supported herself and John."

Mike flipped over the photograph, looking for some kind of notation on the back of it. "Sara, where the hell are you getting all this information?"

She squirmed and looked uncomfortable. "You really don't want to know, Michael."

No, he was afraid he didn't. He'd hoped to have a few more facts to work from, not just Sara's so-called psychic impressions. He flipped through the photographs again. One figure was conspicuously absent.

"There's no picture of John Patrick's father." He hardly realized that he'd mused aloud until Sara answered.

"No, Mamie doesn't like to talk about—" Sara broke off, flushing. She amended. "I—I mean I get the feeling that whoever he was, he wasn't a very good person. An older man who turned out to be married. He seduced Mamie and then left her to fend for herself after she got pregnant."

A tragic story, but not an unusual one. Mike dropped the pictures back in the box along with the rest of trinkets. "This isn't a whole lot to go on, Sara. Are you sure there's nothing else lying around here—a diary or some old letters? Any legal documents?"

Sara shook her head. "If there was anything else left, I'm sure Mamie would have given it to me—that is, I think it would have been there in the box, or hidden away in the closet, too. The only other thing in there is John Patrick's dog."

"His what?"

Sara dove back into the closet and unearthed a small black-and-white stuffed dog, missing one eye, its plush fur dirty and rubbed down to the nubs. It was the same one the kid had been clutching in the picture.

"It was John's favorite toy," Sara explained. "Mamie bought it for him one Christmas because he could never have a real dog here at the inn."

Mike held the ragged, moth-eaten dog up by one ear and grimaced, "I don't think this mutt is going to be much help unless he can talk."

"Well…" Sara began, then stopped, biting down on her lip in a guilty embarrassed fashion that filled Mike with foreboding.

He stifled a groan. "I can almost handle the fact that you think ghosts whisper in your ear, Sara, but please, *please* don't tell me this dog talks to you, too."

"Of course not." Her cheeks colored bright red. "But there are other ways, Michael. Haven't you ever heard of a thing called psychometry?"

"Psycho-what?"

"*Psychometry.* The ability to touch an object and gain impressions or feelings about its owner."

"Oh, that. Yeah, I remember one of the other detectives in the department was always calling in some psychic to fondle the evidence in murder cases." The scorn in his voice showed clearly what he'd thought about such proceedings.

"You used to be a police detective?" But Sara's surprise faded as quickly as it had come. She nodded to herself, murmuring. "Yes, of course you were."

Mike scowled. He hated when she seemed to know things about him without him really telling her. Deflecting the subject away from himself, he demanded, "And you claim to have some of these psychojigger powers?"

Her chin came up in defiance. "A little."

A moment of unease surged through Mike as he recalled the way she'd touched his letter from prison out in the parking lot. Was it possible that she'd been able to tell—

No! She couldn't. Because nobody could do things like that. It was a lot of mumbo jumbo. And to prove it to himself as much as to her, he startled Sara by tossing the toy dog at her.

She caught it awkwardly as he said, "All right. Go for it."

Sara blinked in confusion. "Go for what?"

"Practice your voodoo powers on the stuffed mutt. Use him to tell me what happened to John Patrick."

Sara paled a little when she realized what he wanted. "It's not something that I like to do very often, Michael. It can be rather frightening. And besides, you don't believe in such things anyway."

"What does it matter what I believe?" Mike shrugged. "Maybe I should try to be more open-minded. Go ahead."

Sara's troubled gaze dropped down to the toy she clutched in her hands.

"Unless, of course, you really don't think you can do it?" Mike taunted.

She shot him a reproachful look and her mouth set in a stubborn line. "All right. I'll try. But you have to stay still and be quiet for once."

"No problem." Mike leaned back against the bedroom door and folded his arms, waiting.

Looking decidedly uncomfortable, Sara sank down on the edge of the bed. Taking in a deep breath, she held the little dog tight to her breast and closed her eyes.

Mike experienced a brief twinge of guilt. He didn't know what he was doing, goading her into such a thing. Maybe it was because she was starting to get to him with all this psychic nonsense. Maybe, if nothing else, he needed to make sure he kept his own head screwed on straight.

Any minute now, he was certain she'd open her eyes and offer one of the usual fake excuses. His negative vibes were interfering with her concentration. The moon wasn't in conjunction with the right stars, or some rot like that.

But instead she just sat there, the time ticking by, beginning to tell on his nerves. He was just about to tell her to forget it when a violent shudder wracked through her.

"Sara?" he called uncertainly.

"Afraid," she said in a small voice. "He's so afraid."

"Who is?" Mike demanded.

"John Patrick. There—there's a horrible loud noise and it frightens him."

Although the last thing he wanted to do was encourage this charade, Mike couldn't help asking, "Can you see anything? Are you getting a mental picture? Can you tell where he is?"

"It's not clear. He's outside the inn…I think."

"And what's the noise?"

"A—a siren. And flashing red lights. John senses something bad is going to happen."

"I get that same feeling every time I see red lights in my rearview mirror." But Mike's quip fell flat. Sara was making him uneasy. She'd gone ice white, the contraction of her brow looking almost painful. If Sara was faking, she was damned good at this—the best he'd ever seen. She hardly seemed to be aware of anything Mike said or did, lost in a trance of her own making.

"His mother," she murmured. "John senses something is

wrong with his mother. Mr. Kiefer is trying to comfort him, telling him everything is going to be all right."

Yeah, right, Mike mused bitterly. Where had he heard that one before? Although he'd promised Sara to remain still, he started pacing. He couldn't help it.

Sara suddenly began speaking in a different voice, the soft reassuring tone of an adult trying to comfort a small child.

"It's going to be okay, Johnny. Your mommy has to go away…in—in the big shiny white car."

Big shiny white car, my butt, Mike thought, rolling his eyes. The kid had been six years old. What'd Kiefer think he was, stupid or something? He'd know an ambulance when he saw one.

"But you're going to be taken care of, John," Sara continued, her voice cracking a little. "There is a nice man coming who will help you find a new home."

"No, no!" Sara dropped to a heart-breaking whimper. "Don't want new home. Want my Mommy."

Clinging to the toy dog, Sara began to rock back and forth.

"Sara?" Mike asked sharply. "What the hell's happening now?"

"Gone. Mommy gone. But the gray man is here."

"The gray man?" Mike echoed. "Who's that? You mean someone from the child welfare board?"

"Don't…don't like the gray man. A-afraid. Want Mommy. Can't breathe." Sara drew in a great unsteady gulp of air. "Chest hurts. All squeezed tight."

He knew exactly what she was talking about because oddly enough, listening to her, he was finding it hard to breathe himself. His throat felt raw and dry, like it was closing shut.

"Sara, that's enough," he growled. She was really starting to scare him. "This isn't getting us anywhere."

But Sara didn't even seem to hear him.

"Th-the gray man says I have to be a good boy. But he isn't nice. Wants to—to take my doggie, throw him in the garbage. Says he's too dirty."

"Sara, just stop it!"

"No, no!" Sara clutched the dog to her chest in a death grip, scrambling to cower back against the headboard of the bed. "Can't have him. Have to—to hide my doggie in Mommy's secret place. In the closet."

"Sara!"

"H-have to...." She was trembling all over now, tears starting to stream down her cheeks.

Mike had had all he could take. Striding over, he wrenched the dog from her hands and flung it violently across the room. A terrible cry breached Sara's lips. Seizing her by the shoulders, Mike gave her a rough shake.

"Sara! Snap out of it."

Her eyes flew open wide to stare into his, frightened and disoriented. A ragged sob escaped her, but slowly the haze faded, leaving only blue eyes brimming with tears.

"You—you okay?" Mike asked, gentling his touch on her shoulders.

Sara nodded, color seeping back into her cheeks. She squirmed away from him and rose shakily to her feet. Touching one hand to her face, she suddenly seemed to realize she was crying. Appearing embarrassed about it, she averted her face, trying to get her emotions under control.

"I—I didn't mean to cause such a fuss," she said. "I seldom have a psychic experience that strong. It felt too real."

Mike didn't know what she'd just experienced. All he knew on some gut level was, she hadn't been faking it.

"C'mon, angel," he said gruffly. "There's no sense using your hand when I have this perfectly good jacket you can ruin." He turned her gently, starting to gather her into his arms, but she tried to pull back.

"Oh, n-no. P-please—"

"Hey, it's okay. The local dry cleaner is my bookie. I have a running account." Cupping the nape of her neck, he forced her head against the lee of his shoulder.

She resisted a fraction longer, then wrapped her arms around his neck, burrowing her face deep against his jacket. Cradling her tight in his arms, he made idiotic and totally useless shushing noises, murmuring every fool endearment he could think of. He thought she'd stop crying, but she still trembled.

This was all his fault, dammit. What the hell had ever possessed him into pushing her into trying such a thing? Of course, he'd never really believed this psychic junk would work. He still didn't. Sara was just too...too damn suggestible, blast it! Good thing he'd been able to snap her out of it.

Good thing for her or for you, Parker? his inner voice tormented. That whole bit about John Patrick being scared, the shrill of the ambulance, losing his mom that way. What a bizarre coincidence. It had all struck a little too close to home, didn't it, Mikey boy? Dredging up recollections that Mike hadn't thought about in years, pulling them more sharply into focus. Just what he needed. More lousy memories.

Unconsciously, his arms tightened about Sara, holding her closer. He filled his senses with her, inhaling the fresh sweet scent of her perfume. Was it possible for a woman to smell innocent, like sunshine on roses, summer rain and the first breath of dawn? Sara did.

She stopped trembling and relaxed, her soft, warm curves molded trustingly against him, touching him in some way he couldn't explain.

"S-sorry," she said, her voice muffled against his jacket.

"For what?"

"For acting so stupid."

"It's okay, angel. I do it all the time."

"Y-you mean, you *cry?*"

"No, I act stupid."

Her shoulders shook again, but this time with a watery chuckle. Shifting away from the damp spot she'd created on his shoulder, she rested her forehead against the center of his chest with a tiny sigh.

She fit so nicely tucked beneath his chin. It seemed the most natural thing in the world for him to pillow his cheek against the golden cloud of her hair.

"Sometimes," she said, "I—I hate all these strange things I'm able to sense and feel. I get tired of—of being so different. I wish I could just be normal like everyone else."

"I don't want you to be normal. I like you just fine the way you are."

"You do?" Sara raised her tearstained face to stare up at him, her blue eyes round with wonder and surprise.

"Yeah, I do," Mike said and was surprised himself to discover how much he really meant it.

Sara's lips quivered with a tremulous smile. "I think that's the sweetest thing anyone ever said to me."

No one had ever accused Mike Parker of being sweet before. He wasn't quite comfortable with it, but he pressed a chaste kiss on her brow.

And then another on the adorable tip of her nose. And then both eyelids, her gold-tipped lashes still damp from her tears. And then her cheeks....

He should have stopped there. He really hadn't intended to use this comfort thing as an excuse to put the moves on her. But it was Sara who wound her arms around his neck, offering her lips to him.

What could he do but kiss her back, accepting her generous warmth like a cold, weary traveler coming home? Suddenly he was no longer sure exactly who was comforting whom.

With a boldness that astonished her, Sara threaded her fingers through the thickness of Mike's tawny mane, holding his mouth fast against her own. He kissed her with a gentleness she would never have imagined him capable of, a tenderness that thrilled her to the core.

When his mouth became more insistent, Sara allowed her lips to part, welcoming the hot play of his tongue against her own. The kiss was both fire and magic, going deeper than mere flesh, drawing her straight down into the recesses of Mike's heart, a world of loneliness and aching needs.

Needs she found not so different from her own. To hold and be held, to touch and be touched, to love...

Their lips parted reluctantly as they each paused to draw in an unsteady gulp of air. Mike stared down at her, and for once his eyes were ablaze with a naked hunger, raw and vulnerable.

He kissed her again, more fiercely this time, as though he would offer her all his desire, and Sara accepted, made it her own. Mike undid the band that bound up her ponytail and Sara's hair spilled about her shoulders like a shower of silk. She didn't think to protest, even when he tumbled her down onto the bed.

His fingers found the swell of her breast, caressing her through the sheer fabric of her sundress and Sara moaned softly, pressing herself against the hard length of him, aware of the evidence of his arousal straining against the flap of his jeans. It should have alarmed her, but it didn't, calling forth instead a primitive firing of her own blood.

With increasing fervor, they embraced, stroked, caressed like two people discovering each other for the very first time. And yet, it all seemed so achingly familiar to Sara, as though she'd always known this man's kiss, his touch, always been eager and ready for this moment, waiting....

Mike eased the thin straps of her sundress down, breathing her name with a kind of reverence. He brushed his lips against the skin of her shoulder, sending shivers of heat rushing through her. He shifted her dress down farther still, baring her breast. He cupped his fingers around her, the soft mound molding perfectly to the callused warmth of his hand.

And that was when all hell broke loose. The bed began to shake with a violence that seemed calculated to bring the whole room tumbling down about their ears.

"What the—" Mike exclaimed, his head jerking up sharply, the heat in his gaze replaced by alarm.

Sara gasped, feeling as though a blade of ice thrust between her and Mike, forcing her out of his arms. The bed pitched and rolled beneath them like a small ketch lost in a storm at sea. Swearing under his breath, Mike scrambled off the bed, dragging Sara with him.

They'd barely gained their balance on the floor when the bookshelf on the wall joined in, dancing out a mad rhythm, keeping time with the bed.

"Mike!" Sara cried out a warning as the books came flying off. But she was too late. One hefty tome slammed into the side of his head.

He grunted with pain, reeling away from her. Flinging up

his arms, he deflected several more hardback missiles that seemed to be aimed at him with deadly accuracy.

Only when the last book lay tumbled on the carpet, did the shaking stop. Sara pressed her hands to her heart and drew in a tremulous breath. She'd seen displays of Mamie's infamous temper before, but she never failed to be awed by it.

Cautiously lowering his arms, Mike straightened. Groaning, he rubbed his head and nudged aside a fallen book with the toe of his shoe. *"Webster's Dictionary. Complete and Unabridged."* He winced. "Damn it! No wonder it felt like a ton of bricks."

"Are you all right, Michael?" Sara asked. It was starting to become a familiar question.

"No, I'm not!" he snapped, glaring at the bookshelf and then the bed. "First I nearly break my leg on the stairs. And now I think I've got a damned concussion. What the hell is going on around this place?"

"It—it's Mamie," Sara said, faltering. The room settled to an ominous quiet, but she could still sense something in the air, the chilling breath of an icy disapproval.

"I wasn't making any spook jokes. What's her problem this time?"

"I'm not sure, but...but I don't think she likes you...um— kissing me."

Mike's brows shot up in disbelief. "What business is it of hers?"

Still basking in the memory of Mike's warmth and tenderness, Sara wanted to know the same thing. She called out, "Mamie! You hurt Mike again. Why did you do that?"

Someone had to stop Mr. Casanova there and bring you to your senses.

Sara shivered at the sound of Mamie's voice, but it was obvious from Mike's expression that he had heard nothing.

With a halting embarrassment, she explained, "Mamie seems to feel we were getting too carried away."

"Damn right we were." Mike dragged his fingers through his hair in a gesture of angry frustration, wincing when he came to the bump on his head. "I don't know what the devil came over me. Sorry, angel. You seem to bring out the worst in me.''

"The worst?'' Sara made a feeble effort to smile. "I rather hoped it was the best.''

Mike shook his head. "Give me a woman in a bedroom and apparently I can't be trusted. Good thing that Mamie—'' He stopped, flinging up his hands in disgust. "What am I talking about? There *is* no Mamie.''

Sara stared at him in dismay. After all of this, he couldn't possibly still deny Mamie's existence, could he? Any more than he could deny that what had just happened between him and Sara had been something strange and wonderful. Special.

But apparently he could, for he stalked away from Sara, muttering something about raging hormones. He went over to the shelf to examine it, looking for some logical explanation for the recent disturbance.

Sara's warm glow faded to become an ache of bitter disappointment. She became suddenly aware of her disheveled state, and shoved her dress straps back up on her shoulders, feeling mortified and ashamed.

Maybe Mike was right. Maybe she'd just imagined that there had been anything at all magic about the way they had kissed. Maybe it was nothing but hormones.

Then why did she still feel so shaken, tingling all over just like yesterday when he had kissed her, only stronger?

Just like yesterday.... A peculiar sensation stole over Sara and she clapped her hand to her mouth.

"Oh, no. Not again,'' she murmured. Perhaps it was her eyes she needed to cover. She tried to avoid looking at Mike, but her gaze was drawn to him like a magnet.

In a blinding flash, she seemed able to see straight through the man's clothes again. Only it wasn't just his shirt this time. Everything was gone except his socks and a skimpy pair of black silk briefs. She envisioned clearly the taut calves, the lean, muscular thighs, the broad chest with its golden dusting of hair, trailing over the flat plane of his stomach to disappear into those scandalous briefs. Briefs that outlined far too well an interesting bulge.

"Oh...oh, my." Sara gulped, her face on fire. "You—you have—"

"Have what?" Mike asked, glancing back at her with a puzzled frown.

"You—you have another scar. On your left thigh."

Mike's hand clapped defensively over the exact spot, his frown becoming a full-blown scowl. "Damn it, Sara, don't you start that again. I've been weirded out enough for one day."

"I can't help it," Sara moaned. "I can see it so clear. You got this scar from—" She winced as an image of shattering glass, grinding metal filled her head.

"From an automobile accident. You were driving too fast." Sara's eyes widened at the realization. "Michael! You stole a car."

He squirmed. "Yeah, so what? I used to be a very bad boy. Too bad to live and not bad enough to die and... Hell, Sara! What are you—some kind of a witch or something? How do you keep guessing all this stuff?"

She didn't bother to answer him. It would have done no good. He wouldn't believe her anyway.

"I—I sense a lot of pain," she went on. "But it wasn't as bad as the time you—you—" She drifted toward him, her hand outstretched. "The time you hurt your shoulder."

"Sara, don't," Mike growled in warning, but her fingertips already came to rest on the area where she knew his scar to be. She shuddered as pain sluiced through her—savage, sharp, burning. Mike's remembered pain. But instead of his shoulder, it felt as though the knife had been plunged, twisted in his heart.

Sara felt the color drain from her cheeks. "My—my God. You—you were only a boy when you were stabbed. Just twelve years old!"

"Stop it!" Mike shoved her hand roughly aside.

A jolt of fear rushed through her, not at Mike's rising anger, but at the new image forming in her mind.

"I see the man lurking in the shadows. Terrible, frightening, but I can't see his face unless he steps into the light. He—"

"I said, stop, dammit!" Mike seized her shoulder in a fierce grip. The terrifying image faded, leaving only Mike's eyes, bright and hard with anger. And some other emotion. Could it possibly be…fear?

"Look, Sara, I don't know how you can…or even if you— I mean…that is, I think—" He broke off, his jaw working. "I don't know what I think anymore. But if by some remote, snowball's chance in hell, you really are psychic, I want one thing clear. Stay out of my head, dammit!"

"I don't want to be in your head," Sara said miserably, struggling to ease Mike's grasp, which had become painful. "It's more your fault than mine."

"My fault?" Mike glared, but mercifully he relaxed the pressure of his fingers.

"Yes, I never get visions this clear and sharp when I'm around anyone else. But each time you kiss me that passionately, I'm able to see more and more of you. This time I got all the way down to your black silk briefs."

"For your information, Miss Psychic, I don't wear silky drawers. I don't even own any except for a few pair my ex-wife insisted on buying me, and those are shoved to the back of the drawer. I never bother with them except on days when I'm low in the laundry department, like—" Mike paused, a look of horrified realization sifting over his features.

"Like this morning," he concluded weakly, his gaze dropping to Sara. His hands fell from her shoulders and he ran his fingers over his brow like a man testing for fever. "This— this is insane."

"No, it isn't," Sara insisted. "It's the way you kiss me. It seems to have opened up some kind of channel between us."

"So switch to another station."

"Then stop kissing me."

"Gladly!"

But even as Mike glowered into her eyes, Sara could still feel the currents rushing between them. The attraction that was there whether either of them wanted it or not.

She wondered if Mike felt it, too. She couldn't tell. All she knew was that he avoided her gaze and backed away, saying, "I'm outta here."

"You're quitting the case?" Sara faltered.

"No, I just have to get out of here, that's all. Away from—"

He didn't finish, but he didn't have to. Sara knew what he meant well enough. Away from *her*. Sara Holyfield. It seemed as though Mike would have preferred her a bit more normal after all.

The thought pained her more than she cared to admit. Concealing her hurt behind a hard lump of pride, Sara watched Mike gather up Mamie's jewel chest and tuck it under his arm.

"What are you going to do?" she asked.

"What you hired me to do. Go find John Patrick. Using real, solid detecting methods. The kind of thing I can understand. Hard evidence." He frowned a moment at the bedraggled stuffed dog lying on the carpet and then to Sara's surprise, he scooped that up, too. She couldn't imagine what he would want with John Patrick's most cherished toy. But Sara supposed bleakly that, to Mike Parker, it was just more of his "hard evidence."

Brushing past her, Mike strode purposefully toward the bedroom door. "You coming?" he demanded.

Numbly, Sara shook her head. "I think I'll stay here awhile and see if I can find out anything else."

He angled an impatient glance back at her. "And just how are you planning to get back to town?"

"I guess I can always saddle up my broomstick," Sara said with a trace of bitterness. "Or barring that, there's a local bus line that runs not far from the inn."

Mike looked about to argue with her, conflicting emotions warring in his dark eyes. But then he just shrugged and said, "Fine. Suit yourself. I'll report back to you if I find out anything."

Would he? Sara wondered as Mike vanished out the door. She had a sinking feeling that he'd as soon stick his head in a bear trap as come within miles of her again. She listened to the sound of his receding footsteps pounding down the stairs until eventually she heard the front door slam.

Six

A week passed before Mike Parker ventured back into Aurora Falls. Even then, when he cruised down Main Street, he carefully avoided Sara's shop. But that huge blinking eyeball mounted above her store seemed to follow him like a reproachful stare.

Mike caught himself actually scrunching down farther in the seat of his Mustang as though fearful Sara would pick him up on her radar as he passed by. It had taken him a long time to sort out what had happened at the Pine Top Inn that afternoon and he still wasn't sure he had it straight. He didn't need another close encounter with Sara to confuse him further.

Pressing down on the accelerator, Mike sped down the block to his destination, the Aurora Falls City Hall. He almost missed it, the government offices jammed into a large brick building along with the library and police station. A handy arrangement, Mike thought, where the cops could swoop in right away on all those felons who tried to stiff the librarian out of overdue book fines.

He eased the convertible next to the curb, the sun baking

through the open roof, making him irritable. Hot July had turned into inferno August. His shirt, a wild Hawaiian print in orange and yellow, and his khaki pants were already sticking to him like a second skin. Mike Parker in his *Magnum P.I.* mode, all set to blend in with the tourists. Or make the rounds of area hotels, trying to find that witness that had skipped out on the local prosecuting attorney. Except that, much to his disgust, Mike wasn't doing those nice sane, sensible things.

Those sensible case folders lay neglected on the back seat of his car while he continued to pursue the one case that was obsessing him.

The missing John Patrick.

Shutting off the car motor, Mike stared balefully at the objects nestled on the seat opposite him, the only clues he had so far—a jewel box full of trinkets and old photos and a ratty, little stuffed dog.

He had to be out of his mind. Wasting all this time working for a gypsy lady who made his blood run both hot and cold for the rate of ten bucks a day. Money he never intended to collect anyway.

He'd had so little luck finding anything more about Mamie Patrick that he almost believed the woman really was nothing but a figment of Sara's imagination and that all he was doing was chasing down more figments. But he'd been reassured by Xavier Storm's reaction.

The casino king hadn't been idle these past few days, either. Flexing his influential muscles, he'd done everything, from having Mike's office building inspected by the Department of Health to sending the state commission round to check on Mike's P.I. license.

A subtle threat, a *Storm* warning as it were, that if Mike didn't back off the Patrick case, Storm would do his best to see Mike shut down. Rather than alarming Mike, it filled him with a certain grim satisfaction.

"It shows that I'm already starting to get to the imperturbable Mr. Storm," Mike murmured to his only companion, the stuffed dog. He picked it up and flicked one moth-eaten ear. "Which means that there has to be something to all this Patrick business. Which means that your former owner does exist.''

Mike glanced down at the ragged dog, scowling at some elusive memory the toy kept stirring in him. Could he possibly have had something like it himself when he was a kid? A name hovered just out of reach. Spunky? Spanky? Sparky, maybe.

Yeah, that was it. A stuffed dog named Sparky after some Dalmation firehouse dog he'd read about in a book somewhere.

"Well, I'll be," Mike said, a little astonished with himself. He could recall so little of the details of his early life. So what the hell had ever happened to good old Sparky, he wondered, turning the toy dog in his hands. Probably left behind at one of those endless hotels his old man had dragged him to.

Thoughts of his old man immediately soured the remembrance and Mike tossed the dog back on the seat. That was just one more weird thing about this case—how it kept dragging him back to his own past. Good thing he was getting such satisfaction out of bugging Storm or Mike would've cashed in his chips long ago.

This whole Patrick business was getting under his skin in ways he neither liked nor understood. Just like the woman who had hired him.

Sara.

Mike gripped the steering wheel hard, fighting to keep her image out of his mind. His head was beginning to feel like a damned battleground and most of the time, he lost.

She was always there, sunshine and sweet perfume in the dark back rivers of his mind. Alluring. Tantalizing. Tormenting. He'd lain awake nights, trying to convince himself that the things he'd thought had happened out at that inn hadn't really happened.

He hadn't almost gone out of control and made love to Sara Holyfield on an old bare mattress. No ghost had bounced books off his noggin and Sara hadn't been really able to slip inside his head, the grim wasteland of his past exposed for her to see.

Well, he could still argue himself out of believing in ghosts, but Sara was another matter. He'd almost been able to *feel* her cracking his cynical armor.

All those details she'd picked up—his scars, the car he'd stolen as a punk kid, but most of all, his shadow man. Those details had been all too painfully precise to be dismissed as a lucky guess.

Mike expelled a deep heartfelt sigh. He'd spent most of his life debunking carnival fortune tellers, phony mediums, crystal-ball readers. It was driving him nuts to have to admit, even to himself, that Sara just might be the genuine article.

"It's damned unsettling," he growled, his gaze drifting involuntarily to his stuffed companion. "Well, hell, Sparky. You know what it feels like. She got in your head, too."

Of course, Sara had said it was all Mike's fault, all because of the way he'd been kissing her, and maybe she was right. He had no business to be kissing her, or doing any of the other things he'd been about to do on that bed.

Never get personal with the clients. It was a good rule and he didn't know why Sara kept tempting him to break it. But one touch from her and he was off like a skyrocket. Burning, blazing, exploding with desire. Wanting her with an ache so deep, it scared the hell out of him.

"Maybe she really is some kind of witch, Sparky," he muttered to the dog. "Maybe she cast a spell on me."

Whatever was going on between him and Sara, there was only one solution. Keep working on the case, but stay as far away from her as possible. And under no circumstances, ever, ever touch her again.

"I knew she was trouble from the minute she walked in my office." Mike reached out to tap the stuffed dog on its nose. "Let this be a lesson to you, Sparky. Stay away from dames with faces like angels and bodies meant for sin."

A discreet cough sounded, and for one startled moment Mike almost thought it came from the dog. Then he realized a shadow had fallen over the interior of his car.

He glanced up, chagrined to find a meter maid leaning up against the car door, all crisp and perky in her blue-and-white uniform.

"Excuse me, sir," the girl said. "But the meter you're parked next to is expired. Either you or Sparky is going to have to come up with a quarter or I'm afraid I'll have to give you a ticket."

Mike felt his face firebrick red, but he managed to drawl, "It'll have to be me. Sparky only carries large bills."

The girl gave him a sassy grin and moved off down the street. Hanging his head in his hands, Mike got out of the car. Oh, man, he *was* in a bad way if he was starting to talk, not only to himself, but to a stuffed dog.

Better get down to the business he came for before the damned mutt started answering him back. Mike fed several dimes and a nickel into the meter before turning to the building behind him. City hall. A place where he finally hoped to have some success with his inquiries. So far his luck hadn't been so good. He hadn't been able to locate a soul who had ever heard of the late Mamie Patrick or her kid. No child welfare bureau, no adoption agency, no family, friends, not even anyone who'd worked with her.

He had found a woman who'd once waited tables out at the Pine Top Inn, but that had been after Mamie's time. She had, however, imparted to Mike the startling information that the old caretaker, Albert Kiefer was still alive. The fellow must be in his eighties by now. Unfortunately Mrs. Mcaffee didn't know exactly where Albert was living. The last she'd heard, he owned a little place somewhere just outside Aurora Falls.

Which led Mike on his quest to city hall. The old geezer might have chosen to cut himself off from the world, no longer owning a phone or a motor vehicle, but not even a hermit could escape taxes.

It didn't take long to find what he was looking for among the musty records in the building's basement. One Albert Kiefer had been faithfully paying property taxes on his small patch of ground for the past twenty-five years. If Mike was lucky, he could find this place and be grilling Kiefer about Mamie and her kid, all before lunch. He only hoped the old guy's memory was still good.

Mike quickly jotted down the address and headed back up

to the building's main floor, his sneakers thudding on the concrete steps. The place had a real institutional feel about it. Mike would have wagered his last cent it was a converted school building.

The smell of chalk dust and sweaty gym socks still hung in the air. As Mike paused by one of the white basin drinking fountains to swallow a few mouthfuls of tepid water, the door to one of the former classrooms swung open. Mike half expected the recess bell to clang, but it wasn't a mob of unruly school kids who spilled out. Rather a sedate bunch of middle-aged men wearing conservative suits and an air of self-importance.

Some of the local bigwigs, Mike guessed, winding down an early-morning council meeting. A little coffee, a lot of jawing and a good time was had by all.

Except maybe for the woman who trailed after the men. While the collection of suits disappeared down the hall, she lingered near the door, a pale little thing in a pale pink suit.

Familiar somehow and yet not familiar until sunlight skating through the window outlined her delicate profile.

Sara.

Mike almost choked and spewed out his mouthful of water. His first panicked impulse was to dive for cover, anywhere to escape Sara's uncanny gaze. What the hell was she doing here? Why wasn't she in her shop selling psychic doodads?

But although Mike stood frozen just at the end of the same hall, she didn't even glance in his direction. His gypsy lady was looking most ungypsylike in a tailored suit, her rioting mob of golden curls tamed into a tight bun. She appeared miserably uncomfortable and out of place as she was corraled into conversation with a tall woman who also emerged from the classroom.

Conversation, hell! The tall broad appeared to be doing most of the talking, and for some reason he couldn't say, Mike took an instant dislike to her.

Maybe because she was the sort of female that had always turned him off—too thin and angular, no soft curves, her platinum-colored hair styled as stiff as a wad of cotton candy, her skin perfectly bronzed with a country-club tan. And maybe he just didn't like the way she was in Sara's face, wagging her diamond ring like a rattler shaking its tail.

Mike should have been glad of the diversion. He reminded himself that the one thing he wanted above all else was to avoid running into Sara again. But the more he caught of the conversation drifting down the hall, the more he felt his hackles start to rise.

The woman had a muddy aura. Sara could feel it oppressing her the longer Elaine Jorgensen droned on. She was the kind of person Sara had never understood or known how to deal with. The kind that felt the world had a right to its own opinion as long as it matched with Elaine Jorgensen's. No tolerance for anything unique or different, just the immediate urge to crush it. In another time and place, Sara believed that Elaine would have been the first to point a finger in Sara's direction and cry "Witch."

"...and you must appreciate our point of view, Miss Holyfield," Elaine was insisting.

"I always try to understand everyone's point of view," Sara said quietly. "But—"

"I founded the redevelopment council to give Aurora Falls a much-needed face-lift. No one wants to close your shop down exactly." Elaine's patronizing tone sent Sara quite the opposite message. "Frankly, for your own good, you simply need to try to be a bit more...upmarket."

Sara's grip tightened on her handbag, hanging on to both her pride and her patience. "My great-aunt successfully operated the Omniscent Eye for years, just as it is."

"Er—yes. But frankly, my dear, your great aunt was a wee bit—shall we say—eccentric?"

Shall we just say crazy and be done with it, Sara thought bitterly.

Elaine's lips stretched in her version of a coaxing smile. "Your family loyalty is touching, Miss Holyfield, but you can't be doing all that well. We're attracting a better class of tourist here, the kind that doesn't want odd books and cheap glass necklaces. And frankly, fortune-telling belongs in the carnival not Aurora Falls. No one would blame you if you wanted to sell out and find yourself a decent job. I have always been prepared to make you a very good offer—''

''*Frankly,* she's not the least damn bit interested.''

The blunt refusal cut Elaine off before Sara could even begin to frame a more tactful response.

Sara whirled around, coming almost nose to nose with Mike Parker, a soft gasp escaping her. So much for her sixth sense. How could that much solid male have crept up on her without making a sound? And in that shirt, too. Tropical flowers in all the bold, bright colors of a sunset gone insane.

He loomed behind her, hands planted at his side, lean hips thrust slightly forward in a very aggressive masculine stance. Like a man come looking for trouble and knowing just how to find it, a dangerous glint in his deceptively soft brown eyes.

For a moment, she felt glad to see him, ridiculously glad, as foolish and flustered as a teenage girl with a hopeless crush on the class bad boy. But as she remembered the way they had last parted, Sara quelled the emotion. Salvaging her dignity, she took a step back, putting breathing space between them.

Elaine was the first to recover from her shock. Her cold gray eyes raked over Mike, absorbing the details of his shirt with an expressive shudder.

''And just who might you be, young man, that you presume to speak for Miss Holyfield?'' she demanded.

''Just one of those tacky tourists who likes weird books and cheap glass,'' Mike drawled. ''And who thinks Sara's shop is just swell. A great place to go get your aura fluffed up.'' He angled a wicked glance at Elaine's flat figure. ''*Frankly,* you look like you could use it.''

Elaine stiffened with indignation. Although completely stunned by this unexpected championship, Sara gathered her wits enough to leap into the breach before Mike said anything even more outrageous.

''Uh, Mrs. Jorgensen, this is my—my—'' Sara faltered. What should she call him? Her friend? The detective that she'd hired to poke around in Elaine's inn behind her back? The man who might have become her lover were it not for the intervention of a ghost?

Sara felt her face firing red. "This is my...my Michael," she stammered. "Michael Parker. Mike, this—this is Elaine Jorgensen of Jorgensen's Realty.

"You know. The company that's renovating the old Pine Top Inn," she added by way of warning, hoping Mike would take the hint to watch what he said. She might as well have saved her breath.

Mike let out a long low whistle. "Jorgensen's Realty, huh? The proud owner of Spook Central."

"If you are referring to the story that Pine Top Inn is supposed to be haunted," Elaine said icily, "that's nothing but a scurrilous rumor."

"Yeah, damned nuisance those rumors. Chasing off contractors and throwing paint cans!" Mike grunted as Sara cut him off the only way she knew how, a desperate jab of her elbow straight to his solar plexus.

Elaine's mouth thinned. She made a great show of checking the expensive gold watch banding her wrist.

"You'll have to excuse me, Miss Holyfield. But I'm afraid we'll have to continue this discussion another time."

"Don't count on it," Mike muttered.

Doing her best to ignore Mike, Elaine said, "I have so much to do this morning." She opened the tote bag dangling from her wrist to display a pile of cream-colored envelopes. "The local business association is having its end-of-summer dance again. This year we're hoping to host it out at the Pine Top Inn when the renovations are finished."

"I wouldn't count on *that*, either." Mike chuckled.

Elaine shot him an arctic look and started to move away, but she was stopped by Mike grabbing the handle of the tote bag. "So why don't you save the postage and just give Sara hers right now?"

Because, Sara thought, it was humiliatingly clear that Elaine did not intend for Sara to be invited.

Caught off guard by Mike's direct challenge, the woman

colored a little and then blustered, "Well, I—I just assumed Miss Holyfield wouldn't be interested."

"Why not? She's a local businessman—er—woman, isn't she?"

"It's all right, Mike," Sara insisted in an agony of embarrassment. "I really don't—"

But Mike was already diving into Elaine's tote and helping himself. He dragged out one of the invitations and short of engaging in an undignified struggle to snatch it back, there was little Elaine Jorgensen could do about the matter.

Glaring at him, she snapped her tote closed and stalked off down the hall. As she marched off, her heels clicked out an angry staccato rhythm. Mike watched with a broad grin.

No knight who had just successfully defended the honor of his lady love could have looked more smug or pleased with himself. But before she became too entranced by the image, Sara forced herself to remember a few things. One, she wasn't Mike Parker's lady love. And two, her chivalrous "knight" was the same man who'd been avoiding her for the past seven days.

Mike turned to triumphantly hand Sara the envelope. "Here," he said. "Your invitation to the ball, Cinderella."

Sara shook her head, refusing to take it. "How could you do that, Michael?"

"Do what?"

"Force Mrs. Jorgensen to give me that invitation. I don't make a habit of going where I know I'm not wanted."

"No? Well, you should try it sometime. It can be a lot of fun." But when Sara didn't answer his grin with one of her own, Mike's smile slowly faded.

With a disgruntled look, he crushed the invitation, peering around for a trash can. Finding none, he stuffed it into his own pocket. "Sorry for butting in," he said. "You weren't actually trying to cut a deal with that—er—Mrs. Jorgensen to sell your store, were you?"

"No, of course not."

"Then why didn't *you* just tell her to go to hell?"

"Because I've never been particularly good at that, even with people who deserve it."

"Like me?" Mike demanded.

"I didn't say that." But Sara was surprised to discover how much she wanted to, that she was still hurt and, yes, a little angry over the way Mike had walked out on her at the inn that day.

"What are you doing back here in Aurora Falls anyway?" she asked.

"I'm working for you, remember? You did hire me to take on the Patrick case."

"I remember. But I wasn't sure you did. I haven't heard anything from you for over a week." She didn't mean to sound reproachful or even accusing, but somehow it came out that way, immediately putting Mike on the defensive.

"I told you I'd get in touch when I had something to report, didn't I?" he snapped.

"Yes, you did. So that's why you came to city hall, looking for me?"

"Not exactly. I had to do some digging in the records here."

"And then you were going to come around to my shop?"

"Er—well." Mike squirmed. "Yeah. Sure." But his eyes had difficulty meeting hers.

"What a dreadful liar you are, Mike Parker," she said softly.

"Look, angel, I—" he began, starting to reach toward her, then both his words and his hand freezing in midair. He was obviously unwilling to risk touching her again. After what had happened at the inn, she understood why. What she didn't understand was why it should hurt so much.

"It's okay, Michael," she said with a tired sigh. "I wouldn't want to end up—what was the word?—'weirding' you out again. Maybe you better just call me from a pay phone a nice safe distance away."

"Aw, c'mon, Sara," Mike groaned, but Sara had already started moving toward the exit. Mike cut her off, barricading the door.

"Listen, angel, I didn't—oh, hell, all right, yes, it's true."
He raked one hand back through tawny gold hair that was
already a little wild and windblown. "I was planning to duck
out without seeing you. It's just that—"

"You don't have to explain," she interrupted. "I'm used
to that kind of reaction from people. At the council meeting
this morning, all the chairs around me were pointedly vacant.
You see, you're not the only one who thinks I should be taken
out and burned at the stake."

"Then they're all jerks. And so am I." Mike shook his head
in self-disgust. "I've never been any Sir Galahad where
women are concerned, but I seem to end up giving you a
harder time than most."

"I guess it's more my fault than yours. It's this cursed talent
of mine for getting into other people's heads, invading their
privacy. I must make you very uncomfortable."

"Uncomfortable?" Mike snorted a laugh. After what appeared to be a mighty inner struggle, he blurted out, "Woman,
you scare the living daylights out of me."

This frank confession caught Sara completely off guard. She
gaped at him, wondering when the last time was Mike Parker
had ever admitted being frightened by anything.

"That's—that's ridiculous," she said at last. "You couldn't
possibly be scared of me. You don't even really believe in my
psychic abilities...do you?"

"I don't know what the hell I believe anymore, doll. If
you'd have asked me about this psychic stuff a week ago, I'd
have told you it was all a bunch of bull. Then you come along
and I'm not so sure. I've been going half-crazy wondering if
you could be the real thing."

"Would it be so terrible if I was?" Sara asked wistfully.

"Yeah, because if you're for real, what else is? Ghosts?
Angels? Santa Claus?" Mike gave an uneasy laugh. "Pretty
unnerving ideas for a guy like me whose always had the world
figured out in cold, hard concrete. Black and white."

"Yes, I remember. You said you didn't believe in anything
even when you were a little boy. You wouldn't clap to save
Tinker Bell."

"Hell! I even sat on my hands so I wouldn't be tempted."
Mike jammed his fists deep in his pants pockets as though
afraid someone might demand of him some great leap of faith.

The sight moved Sara in a way she couldn't explain, tugging at her with images of a small, stubborn boy, lost and
unhappy amidst a crowd of excited, applauding children. The
boy who'd grown up into the equally stubborn man standing
before her with the pugnacious tilt to his jaw and the empty
look in his eyes.

Mike Parker with his brash smile and hard-case attitude,
obviously well able to handle himself in any situation. So why,
then, did he inspire in her these urges to brush back the strands
of hair from that obstinate brow, kiss him and make it all
better? Even though she wasn't exactly sure what "it" was.

"I guess I've been sitting on my hands for so long, it's
damned hard to get off them now," he concluded with a shrug
and lopsided smile that somehow went straight to her heart.

"It might not be as hard as you think, Michael." Impul-
sively she stepped forward and tugged at his wrist.

He resisted, saying in a half-nervous, half-joking growl,
"You're not going to go messing with my aura again, are you,
angel?"

"No, I promise that from now on, I'll do my best to stay
out of your head. Unless you invite me in."

He continued to eye her askance, but he let her pull his
hand from his pocket. She curled her fingers around his tough,
callused ones.

"See?" she coaxed. "You're touching me and nothing
bad's happening."

"Yet," he said, but he allowed his fingers to relax just a
little beneath hers. Her hand was soft, warm, silky, but not so
different from any other dame's. Maybe he really had been
behaving like an idiot this past week, dodging Sara, acting
like she had some kind of voodoo power over him.

"Of course," he said, warning himself as much as her, "we
don't want anything happening again like out at the inn, when
we were on the bed and we almost—well—you know."

From the way Sara's face fired bright red, it was obvious she remembered quite well what they had almost *you knowed*.

"Oh, no," she agreed quickly. "We wouldn't want that."

"But if you can keep your psychic radar to yourself, I guess there's no reason we can't be friends."

"Friends would be very nice, Michael." She smiled.

Maybe he could be all right around Sara, Mike thought. But damned if he wasn't starting to feel that crazy, wild tingling again, sparking from her fingertips to his, creeping all the way up his arm.

He would've drawn back his hand, but the thing seemed to have a mind of its own, like his fingers were possessed or something. Clinging to Sara as if he couldn't let go, stroking a slow sensual rhythm on the palm of her hand.

He struggled desperately to get his mind off how soft and delectable her mouth looked when she smiled up at him. How the hell did she manage to keep doing this to him, arousing him, enticing him, *terrifying* him?

He wanted to strip her out of her stiff suit, loosen her hair until it spilled silken gold about her shoulders, set free the sweet wild gypsy lady he'd known for those few precious moments on that bed.

Dangerous thoughts, Parker, he admonished himself, seeking to replace his delicious images of Sara naked with something safer. Like counting nuns in black and white habits. One mother superior, two sisters, three sisters...

Somehow Mike managed to regain control of his hand. Sara issued a tiny sigh that seemed to whisper inside of him, and suddenly he noticed the shadows pooling beneath her eyes.

"So what's the matter?" he demanded.

"What do you mean?" she asked.

He tipped up her chin, studying her closer, not liking the lines of strain he saw feathering that angel-smooth brow. "You don't have to be psychic to tell you've been having a bad morning. Even before I showed up. I suppose that Jorgensen bag and her whatyacallit council's been giving you a hard time?"

"The redevelopment council." Sara nodded unhappily. "They want me to get rid of my eye."

"Huh?" Mike stared deep into her wide, earnest blue ones.

"The huge mechanical eye that hangs over my shop."

"Oh, that." Mike chuckled. "No way. That's one of the most interesting things in this whole boring town."

"Well, the council doesn't share your admiration. They want my storefront to look more like all the others. They're even threatening to get an ordinance passed to make me do it."

"So get a lawyer and fight them. Come out swinging. That's what I'd do."

"I've never been much of a fighter, Michael. Sometimes it's just easier to conform."

"What?" Mike chided her. "Is this the same woman talking who told me she should stop living her life trying to be average and normal like everybody else."

Sara tried to smile, but couldn't quite manage it. "Yes, but I forgot being different can be just as hard. And painful."

Mike wondered who the bastard was who'd been reminding her of that, and then he grimaced. Maybe he should take a look in the mirror.

Sara bit down on her lower lip. "All I ever wanted when I came here to take over my aunt's shop was a fresh start. To feel like there was somewhere I could be myself and still be accepted. To—to belong somewhere. Do you understand at all what I mean, Michael?"

Mike shrugged, but he did understand. Better than he wanted to, her words stirring some answering chord within him. She appeared so fragile, so worn down. All he wanted to do was gather her into his arms and tell her she could hang mechanical eyes all over this damned uptight town if it was left up to him.

A *real* dangerous idea, Parker, he told himself, remembering just where doing the comforting bit had led him before. Tumbling Sara down onto that bed and—

Four nuns, five nuns, six...

Struggling to control his impulses, Mike took a step back,

saying, "Walk out to my car with me. Maybe I've got some news that will cheer you up."

He refused to tell her any more until they were both outside, squinting in the bright flood of sunlight. His words had had a remarkable effect on Sara, the droop gone from her shoulders, the sparkle back in her step.

"You've found out something about John Patrick, haven't you?" she demanded, half tumbling down the city hall steps in her excitement.

"Take it easy, doll." Mike caught her elbow to steady her. "It's nothing that major. All I've come up with so far is an address on that old caretaker, Kiefer."

"Oh, Michael, that's wonderful. If anyone would know what happened to John after Mamie died, it would surely be him."

"If the old geezer remembers. Everyone else sure seems to have forgotten all about Mamie."

"I know," Sara said softly, her eyes clouding over. "And there she is out at the Pine Top Inn, her spirit trapped in those lonely walls. It's rather sad, isn't it?"

"Yeah," Mike agreed, uncomfortable as he always was at any mention of Sara's supposed ghostly friend. Maybe because in some odd way, Mamie Patrick was starting to haunt him, too. It was that damned picture, the last one ever taken of her. The girl's fresh young face, her tragic dark eyes, the tender smile for the little boy she loved so much and knew she wasn't going to be around to take care of much longer.

"My own mother died when I was that Patrick kid's age," Mike murmured. "I don't remember her face anymore. I don't even remember her name."

He winced almost immediately. Now where in the hell had that maudlin thought sprang from?

"I'm so sorry, Michael." Sara pressed her hand over his, her touch warm and gentle, but Mike tugged impatiently away.

"It's not important. It's got nothing to do with the Patrick case," he said, picking up the pace so that Sara had to hustle to keep up with him.

She trailed him back to where the Mustang was parked at

the curbside. Sparky sat waiting for him and Mike knew an embarrassed urge to stuff the ragged toy under the seat as though it actually belonged to him or something.

He positioned himself, blocking Sara's view of the car. "Listen, angel. I've got to get going. I want to try to corner old man Kiefer as soon as I can."

"And you will call me this time?" Sara asked anxiously. "As soon as you find out anything?"

"Sure thing."

"Because I have to report back to Mamie." Sara sneaked a guilty glance around and lowered her voice. "I risked going out to the inn again yesterday to see Mamie and she's getting very impatient."

"She's impatient?" Mike snorted. "Seems to me like she's got more time to kill than the rest of us. Like all eternity."

"But John Patrick doesn't. Mamie keeps sensing that her son is in some kind of terrible trouble."

"Too bad she couldn't also sense where he is. It'd save me a lot of legwork." When Sara started to give him that sad reproachful look, Mike flung up one hand. "All right, all right. I'll call you the minute I find out anything, okay?"

Sara brightened immediately.

"That is *if* I find anything."

"You will. I'm certain of it."

"Your faith in my detecting abilities is real touching, doll," he drawled.

"It's not just your skill as a detective, Michael." Sara cast a shy smile up at him. "Despite how tough you pretend to be, I sense that you're starting to care about Mamie as much as I do."

Oh, Lord! Now where in the hell had Sara gotten an idea like that? Well, now was clearly the time to set the record straight. Tell her the real reason he'd gotten involved in this cockamamie case. Tell her about Storm. Tell her that all Mike was out for was revenge, pure, petty and simple.

Goodness knows, he'd never had any trouble disillusioning people about Mike Parker before. So why had it gotten so hard just because Sara was gazing up at him, her eyes shining and full of trust like she thought he was some damned hero?

Mike opened his mouth only to close it again on a long heartfelt sigh. That was the trouble. Those big blue voodoo eyes of hers. Looking too deep into them was like an out of body experience. From his body straight into hers.

Six nuns—or was it seven nuns—eight, nine...

He needed to get the hell out of here, now. Fumbling around in his pocket for his car keys, he came up with the crumpled invitation he'd filched from Mrs. Jorgensen instead.

"Here. What do you want to do with this?" he asked, handing it to Sara.

"I guess I'll just throw it away." Opening the invitation, she studied the expensive vellum.

"The Aurora Falls Business Association cordially invites you to attend the annual Last Rose of Summer dance," she read aloud. "Dinner to be served in the Pine Top Inn Chandelier Ballroom, followed by dancing in the rose garden under the stars."

Despite her mock formal tone, a unmistakable wistfulness crept into Sara's voice.

"You'd really like to go to that thing, wouldn't you?" Mike demanded.

Sara hunched her shoulders, but Mike wasn't fooled.

"So go ahead and go," he urged. "And the hell with Mrs. Jorgensen and company. You don't want to let the wicked stepmother win, do you, Cinderella?"

She smiled a little at his teasing, but slipped the invitation back in the envelope with a regretful shake of her head. "I wouldn't have anything to wear to an affair that formal."

"So buy yourself a new dress, Cinders."

"And what would I do for an escort? I'm not exactly a sought-after belle here in Aurora Falls, Michael."

"I'll take you," he blurted out, then grimaced. What the hell was he thinking of?

Sara appeared as astonished by his offer as he was.

"Wh-what did you say?" she asked.

Instead of pleading temporary insanity, he actually repeated the damning words. "I *said* I'll take you."

"But Michael...why would you want to do that?"

Why? The woman had a habit of asking the most annoying questions.

"Because..." Because he just loved dressing up in a stiff monkey suit and hanging out with a bunch of bloody snobs like Elaine Jorgensen. "Because I thought it might be fun," he blustered.

When Sara continued to gape at him in disbelief, he tipped his jaw to a belligerent angle. "What's the matter, Cinders? You don't believe I can play the part of Prince Charming?"

"No. That is...yes. I—I—" Sara faltered. She believed in a lot of impossible things. Like ghosts and ESP. Love, romance and fairy tales. She even believed for every woman, somewhere out there waiting was her one true prince. She'd just never imagined that she might find hers wearing a wild Hawaiian shirt and driving a hot red Mustang.

"Of course, there'd be one condition," he warned. "No more of your psychic hocus-pocus stuff."

"N-no, I promise," Sara said, still a little stunned by this unexpected offer.

"Good. Then it's settled."

"Yes, I suppose so. If—if you're really sure...."

Turning toward his car, Mike gave an odd kind of laugh. "Hell! I'm not sure about much of anything anymore."

He opened the car door, only to slam it again. Spinning around, he startled Sara by closing in on her. Seizing her under the arms, he hauled her half off her feet, yanking her toward him for a kiss that was hot, fierce and breathless.

Their lips seemed to meet with all the force of two trains colliding, sending sparks flying in all directions. For a moment, Sara hung suspended, her toes barely touching the pavement; the only solid thing in her world was Mike's hard masculine body crushed to hers, the feel of his mouth, hungry, demanding, possessing.

Then just as abruptly he released her, setting her back on her feet. Sara staggered as Mike pulled away, panting a little.

"There!" he growled. "Now I really gotta go. I'm running out of nuns."

Sara was too dazed to make any sense out of his parting remark. She touched a finger to her bruised lips, still quivering from the sensations Mike had let loose inside her. Passion, tenderness, fire-hot desire. All the things a woman should feel when she'd just been soundly and thoroughly kissed. Nothing unusual.

Nothing unusual? No, there hadn't been. As Mike slipped behind the wheel of his car, Sara started forward to triumphantly point that out to him.

Then it happened.

Not even a niggle of warning this time. Not a tingle. Just a violent flash like lightning tearing a hole through a too-dark sky.

Mike Parker appeared stark naked to Sara's stunned eyes. Beautifully bare, all hair-roughened chest and sinewy thigh, all lean muscle as hard as the gearshift of his car.

She clapped a hand over her mouth to stifle her outcry. Fortunately Mike was distracted at that moment, fitting the key in the ignition, starting up the motor.

By the time he glanced up, Sara had recovered herself enough to step back to the curb. She couldn't speak, but managed a feeble smile and wave goodbye, trying not to look like a woman watching a man drive off, gloriously naked.

"It's not fair," Sara groaned. Mike had just started to trust her, like a lone wolf creeping closer toward a welcoming campfire.

She ground her fingers against her forehead, trying to stop the vision before it went any further, deeper than Mike's sun-bronzed skin and scarred shoulder, invading the vulnerable reaches of his soul.

But it was no use. More images followed like a series of aftershocks. Images too black and terrible for such a bright, sunlit day. A dark alley, a boy's ragged sob, the sharp gleam of a knife, the menacing shadow of a man, his hands stained with blood.

A soft cry breached her lips as Sara thrust the horrifying vision away from her.

"Oh, Mike," she whispered, sagging against the parking meter, clutching it for support. "I'm sorry. I'm so sorry."

She'd already broken her promise. She'd slipped into his head again.

And this time she'd seen the face of his shadow man.

Seven

He had her cornered in the steamy darkness of his office, the only illumination flashes from the neon light across the street. Mike paced in front of Sara, a real tough guy in his fedora and trench coat.

"All right, doll. Time to come clean," he growled. "Breaking and entering a man's head is a felony in this state."

"I didn't mean to do it." Sara pleaded. "I couldn't help myself." She held out her hands, waiting for him to slap the cuffs on. "I suppose you'll have to take me in now."

"Nah. I don't see any need to make this a federal offense. We can square things between us personally."

"How...personally?"

He answered by hauling her into his arms. Shadowed beneath the brim of his hat, his eyes smoldered hot and dangerous as his mouth crashed down on hers.

Yanking off his hat and tossing it aside, Sara buried her fingers in the silken mass of his tawny hair, her lips parting before the demanding onslaught of his kiss. Moaning, she

*raised one stocking-clad leg, rubbing her knee against his
trousers in wanton invitation.*

*Mike's fingers slipped beneath her skirt, following the trail
of her nylon-clad thigh, the heat of his palm searing through
the sheer layer of fabric.*

*But a loud crash sounded in the reception room. He
wrenched away from her, coming to full alert, passion giving
way to tension and fear.*

"You stay right here, doll," he ordered her.

*"But Mike," Sara protested, trying to cling to him. He evap-
orated out of her arms like mist and with sickening suddenness
the room around her seemed to shift and change.*

*She found herself alone in a dark alley. Shivering, Sara
rubbed her arms and called, "Michael?" Silence at first, then
she heard him answer from a long way off, his cry faint and
full of terror.*

*Heart pounding, Sara started to run, but she never seemed
to get anywhere, the alley twisting and turning like some endless maze. Hearing Mike but unable to find him. Until at last
she stumbled down a dead-end street, only to discover Mike
sprawled on the sidewalk. Caught in the glare of a street lamp,
he cast her a look of pure desperation.*

"Get away from here, Sara. Run!" he shouted hoarsely.

*Ignoring the warning, Sara dashed toward him. But before
she could reach his side, a sinister figure melted between them.
The shadow man. Sara watched in helpless horror as he bent
over Mike, raising his knife.*

"Mike, look out!"

A clap of thunder sounded and Sara snapped awake. She
sat bolt upright in bed, her fearful gaze taking in the familiar
surroundings of her wicker furnishings and eyelet curtains. A
summer storm raged outside her bedroom window, a jagged
flash of lightning illuminating the rain-washed panes.

But even that was a more comforting sight than the images
of her recent dream. With a shuddery sigh, Sara sank back
against her pillow. What a horrific nightmare. She couldn't
remember when she'd had one so terrifying, so vivid, so real.

Let that be a lesson to her. Never to go to bed after a late supper of sushi and chocolate cake. Or with a guilty conscience.

Troubled thoughts of the incident with Mike earlier that afternoon sifted through her brain, the same thoughts that had been tormenting her when she'd fallen asleep.

He'd *trusted* her, trusted her enough to offer to take her to that dance, to kiss her again. And what had she done? Invaded his privacy, once more stealing away tiny fragments of his soul he'd never intended to share.

"I didn't mean to do it," Sara groaned, hugging her pillow tight. She cursed the infernal talent of hers for peering into other people's most private pains and secret sorrows. What good did it ever do besides get her into trouble? From the time she'd been six years old and innocently asked the visiting minister about the pretty pictures she saw in his mind of the blond lady wearing the golden tassels. It turned out she wasn't the good reverend's wife.

But Sara imagined that Reverend Thompson's shocked anger on that occasion would be nothing compared to Mike's reaction if he knew Sara had been stumbling around in his head again. What ever was she going to say to Mike the next time she saw him? Confess to the man that she'd been lusting after him in her sleep, that she'd been having nightmares about his shadow?

No, she couldn't possibly tell Mike any of that. Not if she didn't want her quirky Prince Charming with his mad Hawaiian shirt and teasing smile to disappear forever. And Sara was startled to discover how intensely she didn't want that to happen.

But it made no sense this powerful attraction she felt for Mike, this melding of their minds from the very beginning, almost as though...as though their coming together hadn't been a matter of chance, but of fate. And yet they were such different people.

As lonely as her own childhood had been, Sara had always had her books, a thousand fantasies to be lived beneath the roof of her dollhouse, the comfort and security of parents that at least loved her, even if they never quite understood her.

But Mike had grown up a kid of the streets and dark alleys. Shunted between hotel rooms and foster homes, never any place to call his own. Losing his mother at the tender age of six. And his father....

Sara shivered, understanding what had first put the dull light of mistrust and cynicism in Mike's warm cocoa eyes, the remembered pain and scars he'd tried to bury so deeply.

It made Sara long to seek him out, wherever he was, and just hold him, that great tall, gruff man. Cradle him in her arms. To make everything all right, to heal, to give comfort.

But comfort was the last thing a man like Mike would want from her, Sara thought sadly. He wasn't the sort to ever admit he needed anyone, not even if he was dying of thirst in the desert and she stood at his elbow with a glass of water. And it didn't matter, either, that each time he kissed her, she felt all lit up, like skyrockets and pinwheels were exploding in the sky. Because Mike would never see them.

"Only gunpowder and matches, angel," he would likely drawl. "They must be having fireworks in the next county."

No, any relationship between her and Mike Parker seemed utterly hopeless. If fate had decreed their meeting, then this was one time that fate had made a mistake.

Sara needed to stop tormenting herself about the man. Forget him, forget her dreams, forget the desires he aroused in her and try to go back to sleep.

But between the storm and the turbulence of her own emotions, that was an impossibility. Tossing and turning in frustration, she peered toward her nightstand to see what time it was. But the face of her alarm clock had gone silent and dark. She flicked the switch of her bedside lamp and nothing happened.

"Oh, no, not another power failure," she grumbled. Well, that put an end to her usual method of coaxing herself back to sleep by reading a book. Unless she went rummaging for her emergency supply of candles. But if the only alternative meant lying on her back, staring into the dark and trying not to think about Mike, she really didn't have much choice.

Untangling her legs from the hem of her cotton, ankle-length nightgown, she climbed out of bed and minced carefully toward the hall.

The apartment behind her New Age shop was small, consisting only of one bedroom with a bath, the kitchen, and a sitting room that served as both office and the place where she did her psychic readings. Making her way into the kitchen, Sara opened drawers, rummaging around until she found matches and a large wax candle. Propping it in a glass holder, she coaxed the wick to light.

The magnificent bursts of thunder and lightning had stopped, leaving only the rain beating drearily against her windows. No other sound intruded upon the isolation of her apartment except for... Sara tensed, coming suddenly alert, listening. Except for someone hammering against a door. *Her* door to be precise. The front door leading into her shop.

But who in the world would be trying to get into her store at this hour of the night, in the middle of a thunderstorm, for heaven's sake? She tried to convince herself she'd just imagined it when the insistent knocking came again.

Nervously she picked up the candle and crept out of the kitchen, tiptoeing through the sitting room and past the beaded curtains that led into her store.

She never realized it before but the shop was an eerie place at night. The light from her candle flickered over crystals glinting mysteriously in the glass cabinet. The feathered dream catcher swayed overhead and dragon incense burners winked at her with fiery red eyes.

When the knocking thundered louder this time, she nearly leapt on top the cash register counter. Glancing toward the door, she could just make out the shape of a man silhouetted behind the glass, large and threatening. She fought a strong urge to douse the candle and bolt back to the security of her apartment.

"Don't be ridiculous," she admonished herself. "It's probably only someone from the power company or—or one of the neighbors."

The fussy little antique dealer from next door often came stomping over when there was a power failure, as though Mr.

Peavine suspected Sara of practicing some strange mystic rites that drained off all the electricity.

Holding aloft the candle as though it were a talisman to ward off evil, she forced herself forward. The sign on her door pronouncing her shop closed shielded the man's features, but as Sara drew closer, she could tell it wasn't Mr. Peavine. The man appeared too tall, his shoulders too broad.

A sudden hope flared inside of Sara, every bit as irrational as her fear had been. She had no reason to suppose, to even dare to think that it could possibly be....

Her fingers trembled as she reached for the door, but as soon as she touched the handle, she knew.

"Michael," she cried. Setting the candle holder down on top of a display case, she fumbled with the lock and flung wide the door, just as he was raising his fist to knock again. Her breath snagged in her throat.

Swallowed by the darkness and pouring rain, he sheltered beneath her store front's narrow ledge, her huge mechanical eye weeping copious tears down over his trench coat and the fedora pulled low over his eyes. The tough, rough, hard-edged detective. He looked like he'd stepped straight out of her dream.

Her heart turned over but her joy at his unexpected appearance was quickly tempered by remembrance of the way she'd last seen him. Seen too much of him. Visions of Mike driving down Main Street, naked, danced through her head and Sara flushed. She couldn't have felt more guilty than if the police had suddenly turned up at her door—the thought police.

"Michael." She breathed his name again. "What—what are you doing here?"

"Getting wet." He appeared soaked through and his hat had lost some of its dash, the brim wilting a little in the rain. "You gonna let me in, angel, or what?"

"Oh—oh, yes, of course." Sara stepped nervously aside as Mike brushed past her, seeming to bring with him a storm of wind and rain. Sara could feel the tension rumbling off him like claps of thunder.

"Dammit, Sara," he growled, slamming the door closed

behind him. "Do you always fling your door wide open that way in the middle of the night? What if it had been an ax murderer?"

"It wasn't an ax murderer. It was you."

"And how could you tell that? It's black as pitch outside."

"I could tell," Sara said stubbornly, almost defying him to ask her how.

He didn't, turning to grumble at her door instead. "Cheap lock," he said. "I could pick it in two seconds flat. And no security system of any kind. Not even a damned alarm."

"I don't need an alarm. My shop usually isn't invaded in the middle of the night by surly detectives wearing trench coats."

"It's not a trench coat," Mike snapped. "Only a raincoat. In case you haven't noticed, it's pouring buckets outside." Jerking off his hat, he slicked damp strands of hair out of his eyes.

Sara might have been taken aback by his angry tone, but she was sensing something behind all the bluster. Something…lost and uncertain. Whatever had brought the brash Mike Parker to her doorstep tonight, the man wasn't quite as sure of himself as usual.

"So what's wrong?" she asked.

"Wrong? Nothing." He shrugged. "But I promised to let you know what happened with Mr. Kiefer."

"You spoke with him?"

"No-o-o, not exactly." He rubbed the moisture from his chin like a man testing his face to see if he needed a shave. Which he did. His jaw was shadowed with rough stubble, only adding to his Humphrey Bogart look. "I found Kiefer's place, but he wasn't there. His grandson said the old man took off for a spell, fishing, but the kid had no idea where. It'll probably be a couple more weeks before I can talk to Kiefer. This case is turning out to be damned frustrating."

But it wasn't the case that made Mike seem so drained, so edgy tonight. Something else was going on behind those deep brown eyes. It took all Sara's willpower to not probe more deeply.

"Anyhow, that's about it for now," he concluded. "Sorry to disturb you so late. Detectives keep such odd hours, we tend to forget that the rest of the world is usually in…bed."

Mike's lashes drifted down as he took in the details of her nightgown. The garment was certainly demure enough—white cotton, swirling down to her ankles, flowing sleeves that covered her arms, the shirred bodice exposing not a hint of cleavage.

But for a moment, Mike looked at her with a raw hunger, a depth of longing that seemed to reach inside of her, stirring her own desires, touching the most intimate part of her heart and soul.

Averting his eyes, he backed off, saying, "Uh…anyhow, I—I better be going."

He probably should. But as he shifted a step toward the door, Sara cried out, "Oh, no. Please don't."

"But it *is* late and I shouldn't have bothered you."

"It's all right. I like being bothered." She flushed. "I—I mean as long as you're here, you might as well take off your trench coat and dry out a little."

"It's not a trench coat." Mike waved his hat in an impatient gesture and almost knocked several glass cannisters off one of the counters. He frowned, as though for the first time noticing the absence of light. Locating the switch near the door, he flicked it futilely several times.

"Power out?" he demanded.

"It always happens here during storms."

Mike eyed the candle askance. "You got something against flashlights?"

"Yes, batteries. I always forget to replace them." She snatched up the taper and used it to light several other of the large, scented candles from her display case. She hardly knew why she did so except out of an inexplicable sense of desperation. Give Mike enough light and maybe he wouldn't just vanish again, back into the dark and the rain.

He hadn't moved out of the shadows by the doorway, but she could feel the weight of his eyes on her. Turning back to him, she asked softly, "So what really brought you here to-night, Michael?"

"I just got done telling you—"

"No. You didn't come all the way out here in a storm only to tell me about not being able to talk to Mr. Kiefer."

Mike stood there for a moment, fingering the brim of his hat. "And I guess with the power out, I can hardly get you to believe that I was just passing through town and happened to notice your lights on."

"No, Michael."

"Well, the truth is..." He shifted his weight from foot to foot, looking mighty uncomfortable. "Dammit! The truth is you've been in my head again."

He knew! Sara gave a guilty start, whipping her arms behind her back as though caught with her hands full of his stolen memories. She started to babble out an apology when Mike went on. "I haven't been able to stop thinking about you all day."

"Oh." Sara breathed, realizing he hadn't meant what she'd thought.

He drifted closer until he stood inside her ring of candle-light. "You've even been wandering into my dreams, angel." Mike used his forefinger to give her nose a gentle admonishing tap. "Earlier tonight, I dreamed we were locked together in my office. How's that for a hoot? Pretty crazy, huh?"

"Completely," Sara said, but her voice lacked conviction. No, it couldn't be, she told herself. He couldn't possibly have had the same...

"And you were wearing this sexy black dress and nylons with seams up the back," Mike continued.

"And you?" Sara asked weakly. "You—you weren't by any chance wearing your trench coat, were you?"

"It's not a trench coat." Mike frowned down at her. "But yes, I was."

"And—and the only light in your office came from the neon sign across the street. And you pulled me into your arms—"

"And you knocked my hat off and buried your fingers in my hair."

"You kissed me and—and then we..." Sara faltered.

Their eyes met and Mike's widened in alarm. Sara didn't blame him. She felt thoroughly shaken herself.

"Oh, hell!" Mike groaned. But he made a valiant effort at recovery. "It's a coincidence. Just a coincidence. We probably both watch the same old detective movies."

"I never watch any."

"So you're saying we're even starting to share each other's dreams now? What does that mean, Sara?"

"I don't know," Sara said, but she was beginning to have her suspicions about the nature of this powerful link between her and Mike. An idea that she feared he would never accept. One that even stunned herself.

She bit down on her lower lip, trying to puzzle it through. "But wait. We couldn't have been sharing dreams because I was the only one asleep. You were out on the road somewhere..." Sara trailed off as Mike shook his head at her.

"I pulled over for a while because of the storm. I was so damn tired, I nodded off behind the wheel and—" Mike left the rest of his explanation dangling, but there was no need for him to finish.

She was certain Mike would go bolting for the door, and she wouldn't have blamed him one bit. But instead, he rubbed his jaw, asking almost too casually, "So—uh. What'd you think of the dream? The part where we were kissing, I mean."

Sara's face flamed. "It—it was good. Very good," she confessed shyly. Then a chill swept through her. "That is until it all changed and I found myself in the alley."

Mike's face went ashen. "Oh, no. You...you didn't dream that part, too?"

Sara nodded, unable to repress a shiver. "I was lost and couldn't find you, Michael, and when I did...he was there. The man with the silvery gray hair. And his knife. He... It was horrible, terrifying."

"Oh, God!" Mike paced off a few agitated steps, then froze, whipping about to stare at her, his eyes narrowed with deep suspicion. "Wait a minute. How'd you know about the color of his hair? That's never in the dreams. He's always in the shadows.''

"Well, I—I—'' Sara stammered.

Mike strode forward and seized her shoulders in a bruising grip. "You *really have* been in my head again, haven't you?''

Caught. There was nothing she could do but nod miserably.

"Dammit, Sara. You promised me.''

"I couldn't help it. I thought I could. But then you kissed me and— I'm sorry, Michael,'' she whispered.

He released her and said acidly, "So what color undershorts was I wearing this time?''

"None. I—I mean none that I was aware of.''

"So you managed to strip me naked at last. And what else did you see besides my bare butt, Sara?''

Nothing. Nothing at all, she wanted to say. But she'd never been good at deception.

"I saw the man who attacked you when you were a little boy. His face.''

"What about his face?'' Mike demanded.

"It looked familiar somehow. Like—like yours. Only older, harder.''

"Not a very flattering comparison, angel.'' Mike's jaw tightened into a knot. "I always did worry about the physical resemblance, wondering if I was going to end up the same as my old man some day.''

"Oh, no. You never could....''

"Never could what, doll?'' Mike sneered. "Wind up looking like the kind of guy who could plan the murder of his own son?''

Sara winced. She'd guessed the truth about Mike's father from her vision, but it was so much worse somehow hearing him say it flat out that way, his face a cold, hard, bitter mask.

She wished she could think of something to say to him, to take away the pain of her intrusion, to take away even more. That night in the alley. The scar that disfigured his shoulder, the memories that poisoned his mind.

"I'm s-sorry,'' she whispered, the inadequacy of the words

weighing heavy on her heart, bringing tears stinging to her eyes.

Mike watched her in stony silence for a moment, then his anger slowly dissolved. He made a helpless gesture in her direction.

"No, don't do that, angel. It's not worth crying over." He jammed his hands into his pockets, his eyes darkening with some inner struggle. A deep, tired sigh escaped him. "Well, hell. Since you've already found out this much, I guess you might as well hear the rest of it."

"Oh, no, Michael." Sara swiped furiously at her eyes. "I never wanted to force you to share your memories with me."

"It's okay. It's really not that big of a deal. I don't know why I've always been so touchy about discussing my old man with anyone."

Maybe because the memories hurt too much, Sara thought. No matter how Mike tried to shrug and pretend they didn't. But maybe, just maybe he'd carried the pain around buried deep inside him for far too long.

Sara held herself very quiet and still, patiently waiting while Mike roved about her shop, fidgeting with things on the counters as though searching for someplace, some way to begin. He paused before an incense burner shaped like a dragon with scales of iridescent green, purple and gold, a creature more whimsical than fierce looking.

Mike ran one finger along its outstretched wings and gave a smile that was more of a grimace. "I guess my old man was a lot like this fellow here. A lot of flash and color, but when it came down to it, full of hot air. He had a million dreams, all of them involving ways to get rich quick with as little work as possible.

"After my mother died, he dragged me up and down the coast pursuing his schemes. Schemes that weren't always especially...honest. He landed himself in jail for brief spells and I did time in foster homes. But my dad always managed to convince some judge to hand me back over to him. That was one thing Robert Parker was real good at—conning people into believing he was sorry, that he was going to go straight *this time.*"

From the bitterness in Mike's voice, the disillusionment in his eyes, Sara wondered how many times during his boyhood Mike had been conned into believing the same thing.

"Anyhow," he went on, "by the time I was twelve, I pretty much had my hands full trying to keep him out of more trouble. I was worried he'd be sent up for good the next time.

"Not that I cared that much about my old man," Mike added quickly. "I just didn't want to go back to any foster home."

No, Michael, Sara thought sadly. You cared. You cared too terribly much. But she kept this perception to herself, allowing him to continue.

He moved restlessly away from the dragon figure. "About that time, my dad got involved with a real rotten crowd. I'm talking some hard-core criminals here. And my old man started bragging to me about how we were finally going to end up on easy street.

"I got scared stiff. I knew something major bad was coming down and somehow I had to find out what it was and keep my father out of it. So that's what I was doing the night I almost got myself killed. Playing detective."

Sara gripped her hands together, able to envision too clearly the sort of boy Mike must have been, street tough beyond his years, but still a child underneath it all, frightened, vulnerable. Stealing into the night in a desperate attempt to save his father, braving dangers grown men would have flinched from. Her heart ached for that twelve-year-old boy, for the man that now stood before her, his face turned toward the shadows as he relived his darkest memory.

"I broke into the law offices of one of these shady crooks I knew my dad was dealing with. But clumsy kid that I was, I got caught before I could find out anything. By one of Dad's charming new friends. A creep known as Sully 'the Switchblade' Voltano.

"I tried to fight him off, but he dragged me out into the alley behind the office. Then he...." Though Mike's features remained steely, impassive, his hand crept involuntarily toward his shoulder. "He came at me with his knife. But he had the misfortune to stick it to me near this back room where some of the local cops had joined in a game of craps. Sully the Switch got busted. And I got saved. End of the story. Or it should have been."

Mike raked his hand back through his hair, his words coming faster like he wanted to get it all out and be done with it. "The Switch sang for the D.A. like the fat lady at the opera. He said my old man had sent him to follow me that night, put a permanent end to my nosing around."

"By—by having you killed?" Sara whispered, still unable to fully grasp the horror of it.

Mike nodded jerkily. "I guess nobody was going to be allowed to get in the way of Robert Parker's big score. Not even me."

"Oh, Michael," Sara breathed. It all seemed almost too incredible, like the plot of one of those old movies Mike had talked about. But the scar, the dull pain in Mike's eyes were far too real.

After a long silence, Sara asked, "And—and what did your father say to these accusations?"

"Oh, he denied it to the hilt, complete with tears streaming down his cheeks. 'Oh, Mikey, I know I've been a lousy father, but you're all I've got. I love you. I'd never dream of hurting you.'"

Mike gave a bitter laugh at his own mimicry. "Well, the old man had tried to pull off one con too many. No one bought his little performance this time."

"Including you?"

Mike frowned. "That was the pure hell of it, angel. After all his damned lies and cheats, part of me still wanted to believe him. Guess that made me the prize chump of all time."

"No," Sara said gently. "Only a child who wanted to have faith in something every child should have. His father's love."

"Yeah, well, I got over that real fast." Mike squared his shoulders in a brusque gesture. "Besides the little escapade with me, my father also got caught in an extortion deal, pulling off a phony bond racket on some very wealthy people. You can try to engineer the death of your own son, but you better not go messing around with a rich-and-powerful man's money. My dad got sent away to do some very hard time up at Trenton State.''

"Trenton State?" Sara echoed. "Then, the letter that day on the floor of your car..."

"Was from him. He still writes me from time to time even after all these years. I never read them."

But something in the way Mike averted his head gave her the uneasy feeling that he wasn't being entirely truthful about this. She was picking up something. Some dark and disturbing vibes coming from...the envelope that lay damp and crushed in his trench coat pocket.

No! Stop it. She couldn't do this to him anymore. He'd already shared enough of his most intimate secrets with her. Clenching her fists until her knuckles turned white, Sara fought to shut down her psychic perceptions. With great effort, she succeeded.

"And so you've never seen your father again?" she asked. "Not once in all this time?"

"Only in my dreams, sugar. Weird, isn't it? I can't even remember what the Switch looked like. When I have the nightmares, it's always my father lurking there in the shadows waiting with the knife."

Not so weird, Sara thought. One didn't have to be an expert at analyzing dreams to figure it out. The betrayal of Mike's father had scarred him far worse than any weapon could have done.

"Then you have these bad dreams often?"

"Yeah. A load of laughs, aren't they?"

But when Sara shivered, Mike's sardonic expression faded. "I forgot you shared the last one. Do you think that will happen again?"

"I don't know," she said.

He closed the distance between them, brushing his fingers lightly across her brow. "I'm damned if I'm going to have my shadow man creeping from my dreams into yours. If I really thought that was possible, I'd stay awake every night for the rest of my life.''

He tried to make it sound like a joke, but Sara could tell he meant it. The tough guy who swore he was no Sir Galahad would sit up until he dropped from exhaustion, all just to protect her from his nightmare.

She wished there was something she could do to protect him in return. Maybe there was. Acting on impulse, she said, ''There has to be an easier way to keep the nightmares at bay. Maybe what you need is a dream catcher.''

''A *what?*''

Sara answered by unhooking the dream catcher from the wire hook that suspended it from her shop ceiling. She presented the woven rope circle with its decoration of black and turquoise beads and feathers to Mike. ''Hang this in your bedroom and it will catch all your bad dreams.''

''Honey, I'd need one the size of Philadelphia,'' Mike drawled.

''No, really, Michael. According to the old Indian legend, the nightmares are trapped here.'' She pointed to the webbing in the center of the circle.

Mike took the dream catcher in his hands and examined it as suspiciously as some jungle explorer studying a witch doctor's rattle.

''The bad dreams turn into dew and evaporate in the morning sunshine,'' Sara continued. ''Only the good dreams get through.''

''And what if you don't want any dreams at all?''

''Everyone has to have some kind of dreams. Otherwise there's nothing left but the dark.''

''I don't mind the dark, only what's lurking in it.'' He ran one of the dream catcher's feathers between his long fingers. ''So why didn't this gizmo work for you tonight?''

''I don't have one hanging in my bedroom.''

''Ah, I see. This is only something you foist off on unsuspecting customers.''

''No, it's just I've never needed one before. I never really had any horrible nightmares until...until—''

Mike flinched. "Until you met me," he filled in softly.

"Oh, no, of course not. I'm sorry. I didn't mean…" But Sara trailed off, seeing it was useless. How could you reassure a man who wouldn't even admit that he could be hurt?

He handed the weaving back to her. "Thanks, but no thanks, sugar. If I need a good night's sleep, I'd rather rely on a few stiff belts of Jack Daniel's than on what some crazy medicine man did with a leftover ball of string."

"It couldn't possibly hurt anything to try it," Sara coaxed.

"What's the point?" Mike's jaw jutted to a stubborn angle. "What's the point in believing in any of this stuff?" He picked up a box from the counter and smacked it back down. "Fairy dust and dream catchers, rune stones and—and mystic crystals. Why would anybody need any of this junk?" he demanded. "Why, Sara?"

"Why not, Michael?" Sara asked gently. "Maybe you're right. Maybe the things I sell are a lot of junk. But maybe they aren't. Where's the harm in leaving your mind open to a little bit of magic?"

"Because, what happens when you find out the magic's all gone? That there never really was any. You wake up in the morning and there's just four bare walls and you. All alone."

His voice was flippant, but he couldn't disguise the bleakness that crept into his eyes. Appearing discomfited as though afraid he'd revealed too much, Mike turned away from her.

Sara clutched the rejected dream catcher in her hands and ached for him. If there'd ever been a man who needed a little magic, a touch of whimsy in his life, it was Michael Parker. But obviously she wasn't the woman who could give it to him.

They were worlds apart—the little girl who'd harbored fairies and unicorns in her dollhouse and the kid who'd grown up in dark streets and alleys, cutting school and fighting off the hit man sent by his own father.

Sorrowfully, she turned to put the dream catcher back on its hook when Mike growled, "Wait."

When she glanced back at him, he shrugged and said, "Ah, what the hell. I'll take the damned thing. I've got some bare spots on my wall and I guess that Indian doodad would be better than a black velvet painting of Elvis.''

Sara stood frozen in astonishment while Mike moved forward with a belligerent swagger and plucked the dream catcher from her hands.

"How much?" he asked, groping inside his trench coat as though seeking his wallet.

"N-nothing." Sara recovered her wits enough to stammer. "It's a gift, Michael."

"You're going to have a hard time staying in business, gypsy lady, giving things away." He indicated the candles. "And burning up all your stock."

"No harder than a detective who only charges his clients ten dollars a day, plus expenses."

Mike gave her a fierce stare, which she matched, chin up. He caved first, his eyes melting to a warm cocoa, his lips quirking into the familiar grin. She didn't know what had made him change his mind about the dream catcher. Maybe he'd thought she needed the business. Maybe he was just humoring her again. But maybe, just maybe she'd finally reached some part of Mike Parker he'd kept sealed off for years.

No, Sara hardly dared think it. She'd learned at a young age that there was nothing that chased magic away quicker than questioning it too closely.

And there was definitely magic in the way Mike was looking at her now, candlelight reflected in his eyes. Or maybe the flames she saw there came from some deeper source. She felt that strong pull she always felt when Mike stood so close to her, tension humming between them like an old and familiar song. Like in a half-remembered dream. Or maybe even in another lifetime.

Staring into his eyes, she found herself drifting closer, scarcely realizing what she did. The dream catcher tumbled to the floor as Mike reached for her, drawing her into his arms.

Time seemed to stop, the whole world going still as his mouth descended to meet hers. His lips covered hers, gently at first and then with greater insistence, the hot play of his tongue teasing hers. It was the kind of kiss for making magic, stoking desires, stirring dreams.

Mike strained her close, closer to his heart than he ever let anyone come before. Burying his face in her hair, he breathed a long sigh, wondering what insanity was stealing over him.

In the brief time he'd known her, his gypsy lady had involved him in some of the damnedest situations. Ghost hunting, mind reading, dream sharing. And now this. Midnight confessions, revealing to her vulnerabilities he'd never shown anyone before. Dark sweet embraces stolen by candlelight, making him hunger after her so badly, his hands were shaking.

As he locked his arms about her even tighter, whispering kisses upon her upturned face, her eyelids, her cheeks, her nose, her chin, all this craziness was starting to feel so right.

Like maybe it was the rest of his whole rotten world that was insane. The endless cases of cheating spouses, insurance frauds and accounting scams. The murky memories being stirred up by his hunt for the Patrick kid. His petty quest to get back at Xavier Storm for messing with his ex-wife. The letter crushed in his pocket, the one he'd been a fool to ever open...

"Mikey, I'll be getting out soon...."

The shadow man of his nightmares was threatening to spill back into his days, and instead of planning how he was going to handle it, he'd driven aimlessly around for hours with only one thought in his head.

Sara... He needed to see Sara. To feel the comfort of her warmth, her smile, her touch. Mike Parker, the tough guy, who'd spent most of his life running away from everyone— never *to* anyone.

Now here he was crushing her in his arms, kissing her like he couldn't bear to ever let her go. But it was wrong. All wrong. Somehow he had to find a way to stop before he blazed them both down the trail to disaster.

It took every ounce of his will, but he managed to ease her gently out of his arms.

"It's late," he said huskily. "I—I should be going."

"No!" Sara's cry seemed almost involuntary. She clutched

at the front of his coat. "I—I mean you don't have to. You could...stay."

There was no mistaking her meaning. When she gazed at him, her face was suffused with the delicate flush of passion, the glow of a woman waiting, willing to be loved. He'd never realized that desire could be such a pure and simple thing, almost holy when shining from a pair of deep blue, earnest eyes.

She was offering him everything he hungered for, and he didn't know why he didn't just reach out and take advantage of it. This hesitation was something new for him. Mike Parker, in his gentleman mode. Until tonight he'd never known he'd had one.

Swallowing thickly, he gathered her hands and put them away from him. "That wouldn't be a very good idea, Sara. My staying."

"Why?" she whispered. "Don't you want me?"

A sound escaped Mike, somewhere between a laugh and a moan. "Want you? Angel, I want you so bad, it scares me, but I've got no way of protecting you."

The color in her cheeks heightened. "You don't have to worry about that. I take the Pill. For medical reasons."

"That wasn't the only kind of protection that I meant." He cradled her face in his hands. "Sara, you're the kind of woman that has 'forever' written all over you. And me... I've never been able to make anything in my life last longer than a cheap plastic ashtray."

"I know that," she said with a sad smile. "And I'm not asking for forever, Michael. Just tonight." Catching one of his hands, she pressed a kiss into his palm, the soft, warm pressure of her lips sending a powerful rush of heat licking through his veins.

Mike stifled a groan. She wasn't making this any easier for him. She slipped her arms around his neck, nestling close to him, making him painfully aware of every soft curve draped beneath that sheer white nightgown.

"Sara, Sara." He sighed. "You're playing with fire, girl. Look what's already happened between us with just a few kisses. If I make love to you, you could have one helluva psychic hot flash.''

"I've already seen you naked. How much further can I go?"

"A lot further.'' he said. "What if you end up with the whole works this time? All of me. Body and soul. My soul's not a fit thing to offer any woman, let alone an angel like you.''

"Why don't you let me be the judge of that, Michael?'' Sara skimmed her fingertips along the side of his face, the gesture more tender and loving than any he'd ever known.

Easing away from him, she picked up a candle and held out her hand. "Please stay. Stay the night with me.''

No pleading, no blatant seduction. Just a simple request that cut straight to his heart. Sara stood before him, her winsome face and golden hair haloed by the candlelight, her lips soft and inviting. His gypsy lady. All the warmth that had always been missing from his black-and-white world. Would it be the worst thing that he'd ever done to steal a little of her sunshine for a while?

Possibly so, but he was too new at this being-noble business to hold out any longer. He hesitated one moment more before taking the biggest risk of his life.

Mike Parker reached out of the shadows and took Sara's hand.

Eight

Candlelight shed a soft glow over the white eyelet and lace of Sara's bedroom, daunting Mike with the sheer femininity of it. She settled the candle holder on her dresser and turned back to face him, eyes shining, expectant.

This is the moment you're supposed to swoop her into your arms and carry her over to the bed, stupid, the more impatient part of his anatomy urged him.

Instead, he stood as if frozen to the carpet, awkward and uncertain. What the hell was the matter with him? He'd known what to do with a woman in a bedroom since he'd been seventeen. Pounce, peel off her clothes and get down to it.

But as usual, it was going to be different with Sara. Maybe, he was amazed to discover, because he wanted it to be. She drifted toward him, something endearingly innocent, almost childlike about the way her bare feet peeked out from beneath the hem of her nightgown. But the body draped by that sheer white cotton was definitely that of a woman, all soft enticing curves, the dusky aureolas of her breasts, intriguing shadows beneath her bodice.

Mike's mouth went dry. He'd only ever known the black lace teddy kind of female like his ex-wife. He'd had more pasties and fire red G-strings flaunted at him than a country hick lost in a strip joint.

How strange then, that it was Sara, in her angel white nightie, capable of arousing such hunger in him, such an indescribable longing, it was almost enough to make a grown man cry.

She came to a halt in front of him, running her fingers lightly up the lapel of his coat.

"Well, Mr. Parker," she whispered, her smile gently teasing. "Aren't you ever going to take off your trench coat?"

"It's not a—" he started to deny, then gave it up with a wry grin. "All right, all right, you win. It's a damned trench coat. Mike Parker in his Sam Spade mode." Feeling sheepish, he quickly undid the belt and buttons, stripped off the coat and flung it to the far corner of the room.

"Guess I read too much Mickey Spillane and Ray Chandler as a kid. Always pretending that I could grow up to be the same kind of tough-guy detective."

"I'm glad that you had some make-believe in your life, Michael," Sara said with one of those tender looks he almost found unbearable. "I used to play pretend about a lot of things when I was a little girl."

"Oh, yeah?" He slipped his arms about her waist, drawing her close until she fit nicely beneath his chin. They made a strange contrast reflected in her dresser mirror. Sara in her white nightgown, a soft tumble of blond curls cascading down her back. Like someone straight from heaven. Him in his faded jeans and black T-shirt, unshaven jaw and windblown hair. Like something that had been tossed back from hell.

He grimaced, avoiding the sight by resting his cheek next to her temple and nuzzling a kiss against her brow.

"So, angel," he murmured. "What kind of things did you pretend when you were a kid? The usual girl stuff, I bet. Knights on white chargers and the handsome prince bit?"

"No. I used to go hunting for fairies in the rose garden."

Mike groaned. "I might have known."

"And unicorns."

"A horny what?"

"A unicorn." She glanced up at him, her eyes half-laughing, half defying him to tease her. "You know. The mythical horse with the horn growing out of its forehead that can only be captured by a virgin."

"There must be a real shortage of those these days."

"Unicorns?"

"No, virgins." But as he gazed down into her upturned face, the teasing light in his eyes darkened to something more intent.

When he bent to kiss her, Sara couldn't help reflecting that there was going to be even one less virgin in the world after tonight. But that was the last thing Mike needed to know right now. Despite all his efforts at banter, Mike seemed skittish about being with her.

Which was odd. Considering it was her first time, she was the one who should have been nervous. But she had never felt so calm, so sure of herself. It was as though she'd been waiting for this night all of her life. Maybe even several lifetimes.

Her lips trembled beneath the warm pressure of his and she closed her eyes, threading her fingers through his hair, savoring the hard, unyielding strength of his body pressed to hers.

Mike broke off the kiss, resting his forehead against her with a deep sigh. "Sara, are you really sure this is what you want? Because we're getting close to the point where I'm not going to be able to stop."

"I don't want you to stop," she said.

Passion warred with a gentleness rarely seen in Mike's rough-hewn features. "This is going to sound really dumb, angel, but I keep worrying I'm going to hurt you somehow. Destroy all that magic you believe in so fiercely."

"You can't." She laughed. "I have too much of it. So stop worrying, Mike Parker."

What a time for Mike to turn so solemn and serious on her. How could she convince this impossibly skeptical man that she knew what she was doing? That she was more sure about this than she'd ever been about anything in her whole life, even when she had flung everything aside to come here and take over her aunt's shop?

Sara could think of only one way. Stepping back from him, with fingers that trembled slightly, she raised the hem of her nightgown and tugged it off slowly over her head.

As the candlelight skimmed over the outline of her bare breasts, she saw Mike swallow deeply. She knew more about the arts of the rune stones and crystals than she did about seduction, but she had a feeling she was on the right track.

With a gesture that was simple and direct, she reached down to her lace-trimmed satin underpants and dropped the last of her modesty to the bedroom floor.

Mike's eyes dilated. He shuddered as though a sudden shock wave passed through his body. Sara trailed her hand down the breadth of his chest and she could feel the irregular thumping of his heart.

"Tonight," she whispered, "let me make some magic for you."

Her mouth curving into a soft, inviting smile, she pushed aside the tangle of sheets and coverlet and stretched out on the mattress, her hair fanning across the pillow. She gazed up at him with a look of such longing, such trust, Mike felt something constrict in his chest.

If he wasn't such a selfish bastard, he'd leave now, before he did end up tainting her somehow with his dark cynicism, his bleak outlook on the world. But he was already too far-gone, held spellbound by the delicate perfection of Sara's naked form, the sweet promise in her eyes.

Eagerly, he started to lower himself to the bed when the thought occurred to him that he was somewhat overdressed for the occasion. Quickly, clumsily, he yanked at shirt, jeans, shoes, boxer shorts, sending the garments flying to the carpet.

He straightened to find Sara studying him through half-lowered eyes, a dream-ridden expression suffusing her flushed features.

"You're a beautiful man, Mike Parker," she murmured.

"Why, thank you, ma'am," he said. "I try to keep fit." But behind his teasing drawl, he felt a strange sensation sting his cheeks. He was blushing! He couldn't remember when the last time was that he'd been embarrassed about stripping to the buff in front of a woman. Well, hell, he never had been.

But none of them had ever told him he was beautiful before. Clod! his inner voice railed. That was the kind of thing he should have been saying to her.

He eased himself down on the bed beside her, the mattress giving beneath his weight. Sara turned and curled into his arms like she belonged there, like she always had. The feel of her smooth, bare skin nestled close to him sent a charge through him like an electric current.

But he forced himself to simply hold her for a moment, wishing for once that he wasn't such a wise guy. That he knew how to say some of the tender things a woman liked to hear at such a moment, some of the things he was thinking. Like how lovely she was. So lovely she made him feel like some humble mortal who'd strayed into the realm of a golden-haired enchantress. That he didn't have much to offer by way of dreams or magic, but if she could find anything left in his jaded heart, she was welcome to it.

Incredible thoughts for a jerk like him. Small wonder he couldn't seem to get any of them off the tip of his tongue. Lacking the words, he expressed himself the only way he could, with his touch, his kiss, the language of his body. Caressing back her hair, he cupped the nape of her neck, easing her forward to cover her mouth with his own. Her lips were soft and welcoming beneath his, parting like velvet petals, inviting him to taste of her honeyed warmth. His tongue joined with hers in a rhythm that was a tantalizing prelude to the mating yet to come.

Sara arched blissfully against him, each movement, each shift of her body pure sweet torment, bumping up his rising temperature another notch. Her small slender fingers fluttered over him, timidly at first, then growing bolder by the minute, exploring the contours of his chest, his muscles going taut beneath her caress, matching the hardness he felt stirring elsewhere. The woman always had been able to set him off with the merest touch, but he didn't want this to happen between him and Sara too hot and fast. He wanted... The most corny thought he'd had yet filtered through his astonished brain. He wanted this night to last forever.

He sucked in his breath hard when Sara's questing fingers strayed lower, over the flat plane of his belly, grazing against his rigid shaft. His pleasure was sharp, exquisite when she touched him there, and it took all his will to capture her hand, stop her.

"You—you don't want to do that just yet, angel," he breathed. "Unless you want the fireworks going off early." He winced as soon as the words were out of his mouth. Oh, right, Parker. Now there was a nice tender thought to whisper in a woman's ear.

But Sara only smiled, a hint of unexpected wickedness creeping into her blue eyes. "That's exactly what I want to do. Set off so many fireworks even you have to see them, Mike Parker."

She pressed him on to his back, levering herself above him. Nipping playfully at the line of his jaw, Sara trailed a line of soft kisses down to his chest. He lay back, letting Sara weave her woman-magic over him, savoring all the sweet, warm, wonderful textures of her, her fresh, clean scent, the silky brush of her hair tumbling about him, the soft weight of her breasts grazing his chest, the gentle stroke of her hands, the hot moisture of her mouth.

It was a new thing for Mike, surrendering control of the situation. It was new for Sara, being the one in charge. She was more amazed by her own boldness than she'd ever been by the discovery of her peculiar psychic powers.

Magic. Fireworks. Rash promises for a woman to make to a man, especially a woman as inexperienced at this sort of thing as she was. Yet she felt guided by an instinct as strong and mysterious as the sensations awakening in her own body. Somehow she knew exactly what Mike needed—where to be touched, caressed, loved—for his needs were her own.

She was fascinated by the play of his muscles beneath his skin, his body so different from hers—coarser, rougher, harder. His very maleness excited her, making her more keenly aware of her own femininity, making her want to melt into him.

Mike tensed beneath her touch, his breath quickening, and Sara gloried in her power. He often teasingly called her his gypsy lady and she felt like one tonight, as wild as any sultry spirit who had danced, swaying barefoot around the flickering heat of a campfire. Witch. Siren. Temptress.

It was only when her fingers strayed too near the scar on his shoulder that she faltered. She'd never seen the jagged, raised streak of flesh outside of her visions, and the sight of it flooded her with tenderness, making her heart ache for him. No matter how tough he pretended to be, that one small mark on his skin would always be a reminder of his vulnerability.

She bent to kiss the scar, but Mike stopped her.

"Don't do that, angel," he said.

"Why not?"

"Because it's ugly."

"Not to me it isn't." She pressed her lips against his scar in a kiss that was more gentle than he'd ever imagined a kiss could be.

He felt something stir, tighten deep inside him in the region where he supposed his heart should have been. A warm, glowing feeling, deeper, different from the heat of desire. When Sara raised her head, it wouldn't have surprised him to find that she'd exercised some of her strange gypsy power on him and the scar was gone, healed.

It was still there, but somehow it didn't seem quite as ugly as before, as though some of the pain connected with it, the remembrance, had been conjured away.

Maybe because at the moment he was unable to remember the existence of anything in the world but Sara. He brushed back the golden sheen of hair from her face, capturing her mouth in a searing kiss. Although his body was more than ready, aching with the need to bury himself deep inside her, it wasn't enough. He wanted her just as hungry, just as eager.

"My turn, now," he murmured against her lips. "Let's see if I can make a little magic for you."

He sought and found her breast, possessing it in the callused warmth of his palm, molding, teasing, gently abrading her nipple in a way that sent heat singing through her veins. Sara thought her body had been responsive to Mike's touch before, but as his fingers began a slow languid exploration of all her curves, her most intimate places, she fast realized how naive she had been.

He kissed the madly pounding pulse at her throat, his breath coming hot and quick between the valley of her breasts, moments before his lips fastened upon the bud of one nipple, enveloping that most sensitive point with the heat of his tongue.

Her whole body shuddered at the unexpected pleasure of this contact. She'd never given much thought to the mysteries of her own body. But Mike was unfolding those mysteries one by one, his hand skimming over the smooth curve of her stomach, delving lower still. Her muscles clenched in involuntary anticipation as his hand insinuated itself between her thighs, seeking out the tender spot from which all the fire, all the need seemed to radiate.

The spark of pleasure was so intense, Sara bucked upward bringing herself in full contact with Mike's questing fingers. And she had imagined she could show this man anything about setting off fireworks. He'd probably been lighting the matches ever since puberty.

"Oh—oh, my," she gasped. "You—you have very gifted hands, Michael."

She immediately felt foolish, but Mike chuckled.

"Yeah, I had a music teacher once who said I should take up the violin, but I was too busy learning other things."

He demonstrated by setting up a rhythmic stroking, his fingers moving lightly, deftly over the sensitive nub. A low moan escaped Sara and she dug her hands into the mattress.

Mike had never realized a man could find such pleasure just watching the face of the woman he was making love to. The flush of passion bloomed along the delicate arch of Sara's cheeks, burned bright in her eyes.

"Oh, Michael," she panted. "I—I want—"

"What do you want, Sara?" he whispered.

"I—I want you. I want you to be part of me."

"I already am." Mike wasn't sure whose husky voice had breathed such wildly romantic nonsense. He was startled to realize it was his, equally startled to discover he almost believed it was true. That he *was* linked to Sara in some undefinable way, and would have been even if they'd never kissed or touched. If only their eyes had met across a room.

Crazy thoughts, he told himself, when the only sort of joining he really understood was the kind his body cried out for now. She buried her fingers in his hair, breathing out his name in a ragged plea he could no longer deny, the urgency too like his own. He answered her with a kiss, drawing her tight into his embrace, filling his hands with her softness, his heart with the beauty that was Sara.

Levering himself above her, he parted her thighs gently, preparing to ease himself inside. She was moist and ready for him, but he'd never known any woman to be so tight. A vague suspicion filtered through his head. Could it be possible that she was still—

The thought was gone the next instant as she clamped her hands tight around his hips, arcing upward, making their union complete.

Sara stifled her cry against Mike's shoulder. The brief moment of pain she'd experienced at his entry ebbed, leaving her lost to the sensation of Mike filling her with his pulsing heat. Strange, wonderful.

It felt so right, so natural that their bodies should become one, no more barriers between them, two halves of the same whole. As Mike began to move inside her, the initial pain gave way to a throb of pleasure. Sara writhed beneath him, eyes half-closed, Mike's face flashing before her, his eyes dark, storm-ridden.

Mike tried to go slow, be gentle, but Sara wouldn't let him. She matched each powerful thrust of his body, pleading, urging him on, her kisses hot, feverish, demanding he hold nothing back—not just the rhythms of his body, but of his very heart and soul.

Every sense she possessed was attuned to him so it didn't

surprise her when her world exploded in a flash of light. But there were no terrifying psychic images this time, only a single revelation crystal clear.

Love... She loved Mike Parker, would love him forever.

With a muffled sob of joy, Sara clung to Mike tightly as her passion reached its peak, shattering inside of her, leaving her trembling.

It was impossible, Mike knew that, but he could swear that he realized the exact moment when Sara found her release. It was the same moment his own pleasure intensified to the point of pain. The feeling was too strong to resist, and he had to surrender, the sweetest surrender he'd ever known. His entire body shuddered as he spilled his seed deep inside her.

Panting, he collapsed back to the mattress, the two of them still clutching each other like people who had just survived a storm. As he struggled to catch his breath, he almost felt that he had.

He could hardly believe what had just taken place between him and Sara. Sex was usually a hit-and-miss affair. No two people ever got it so right on the first try...so perfect. It was like they'd done it together dozens of times, knew each other's bodies better than they did their own.

You couldn't even call it sex. It was—hell, he didn't know what it was. Magic. Fireworks. He could swear to God he'd seen fireworks and—

And he could also swear if he believed that, then he'd lost his mind at last. But at the moment, with Sara cradled close in his arms, he didn't even miss it.

Her head burrowed deep against his shoulder, he could feel the mad race of her heart, slow to beat in a more steady rhythm along with his own. All was silent except for the soft stir of her breathing and the continued tap of the rain against the windows.

He pressed a kiss into her hair, his heart so curiously full, he felt he ought to say something, but damned if he knew what.

''The power's back on,'' he murmured at last, noticing the

alarm clock light blinking. He almost groaned aloud. Another great romantic one-liner from Mike Parker.

Sara shifted enough to look, then nestled back against him. "So it is. But I don't care," she said in a voice of muzzy contentment. "I still prefer my candle."

Strangely enough, so did he. He'd never noticed before what candlelight could do for even the simplest of rooms. Transform it into a place of romance or sinister shadow. Sara's candle seemed to do a little of both, giving him the feeling of being lost with her in some intimate glowing circle while holding a very dark world at bay.

He wanted to thank her for giving him one night of peace away from his blasted nightmares, from the horrible implications of the note crushed in his coat pocket. But when a heavy sigh escaped her, he wondered if it had been quite as good for her as for him.

"You okay, doll?" he asked. "I mean, was *it* okay for you? I mean...." He faltered, tied up into knots by his own blasted clumsy tongue.

She smiled mistily up at him. "Oh, yes, *it* was wonderful. I was only thinking something...silly."

"Tell me," he insisted, giving her shoulders a gentle squeeze.

"I was just wishing that it could have been as special for you as for me. That it was your first time, too."

"First time for what?"

"N-nothing." Looking as though she already regretted her words, Sara nuzzled her face back in his shoulder.

Still hazy from their recent lovemaking, it took a moment for his brain to focus. Then it did so with dawning horror.

"You—you're not trying to tell me it was your first time for— That you were still a—"

He shifted, trying to peer into her face. Sara shrank deeper against his chest.

"Sara! You were! You were still a virgin!"

"Was it illegal?" she asked.

But Mike couldn't even begin to joke about it. He sat up so abruptly, Sara's head plunked down on the mattress. Dragging his hands back through his hair, he muttered, "There was a moment when I almost suspected, but I thought, nah, impossible. You've got to be almost…"

"Twenty-five years old." Sara winced. "I told you I've always been a little different."

"So what the heck were you doing? Saving yourself for the right man."

"Something like that."

"Then, boy, did you make a wrong turn, sister."

"I don't think so." Sara tugged gently at him, until he shifted to lie uneasily back down beside her. "It's no big deal, Michael," she said. "Though I guess now I will have to give up on ever catching that unicorn."

She was teasing of course, but Mike squirmed, feeling as if he had cheated her out of something. He didn't know quite what. Maybe just that her first time should have been more romantic. Moonlight and roses. A guy spiffed up in his best suit and smelling of expensive cologne. The *right* guy. Mr. Prince Charming himself.

No matter how incredible a job Sara did of kissing Mike Parker, in the morning he was still going to be a toad.

"You should have told me," he grumbled.

"But then you might have stopped," she said.

"No." Mike knew himself better than that. He couldn't have been that self-sacrificing. Toads seldom were.

"But I could have been more careful, tried to make it better for you."

"It couldn't have been any better," she said, rubbing her fingers lovingly over the expanse of his chest.

His male ego should have been flattered. He should have made some snappy comeback and just let it go. But somehow being Sara's first lover seemed to carry such an awesome weight of responsibility and he wasn't sure he could handle it.

When he fell silent, staring up at the ceiling, Sara pressed closer, coaxing him anxiously. "Come on, Michael. I can't be the first woman you've ever known that was—er—inexperienced."

"I don't usually get my dates fresh out of the convent, Sara. Most women I've known I picked up in strip joints or bars."

After a brief hesitation, Sara asked, "Is that where you met your ex-wife?"

"No, I found her in a cake."

He almost laughed at Sara's look of confusion. "I was at this wild bachelor party and Darcy was the exotic dancer who popped out of the cake. I must have been drunk, but I took one look at her and felt like I got hit with a ton of bricks. After a whirlwind weekend together, we ended up married."

"It sounds terribly romantic," Sara said wistfully.

"I don't know about that. We were a lot alike. Darcy had had a pretty rough childhood, too. Both of us were smart street kids. I guess we understood each other. We had a lot of laughs. Until the cake ran out."

Until Xavier Storm had come along. But the thought didn't carry its usual sting tonight. In fact, lying here with Sara, none of what had happened with Darcy seemed important at all.

Sara hugged a pillow to her breast, looking pensive, and Mike cursed himself, wondering how much more of a dope he could be tonight. Going on about his ex-wife to the woman he'd just made love to.

Tugging the pillow away from her, Mike pulled Sara back where he liked her best, tucked all safe and warm in his arms.

"And what about you, angel?" he asked. "You gonna tell me there wasn't ever any guy who tempted you to part with your virtue before I came along?"

He felt her smile against his shoulder. "I suppose there might have been one. I came close once with a bank officer I worked with. Wallace Hatcher."

"Sara, no woman could come close with a guy named Wallace Hatcher."

"He was a very good man, Michael. A perfect gentleman, something rare in this day and age. Very steady and kind."

Neither of which could be applied to Mike Parker. He was annoyed to discover he felt a surge of jealousy over this bozo.

"So what happened?" he growled. "Why didn't you end up marrying Mr. Perfect?"

"We were almost engaged, but well, that's when I had my big revelation and I decided to come out of closet, psychically speaking. Poor Wallace didn't quite know how to handle it."

"So the creep dumped you?"

"No, I let him go." She levered herself up a little to look at him, her eyes sweet and serious. "You see, Michael, I already have to deal with so much skepticism. I couldn't possibly marry a man who didn't believe in the things I do, accept me for what I am."

"But still, no matter what he believed, this Wallace jerk wouldn't have let you send him away if you two had really been in love with each other."

"But I thought you don't believe in love, Michael. Do you?" she added softly.

"Well, I..." Their eyes met, a look stealing into his that took Sara's breath away. But the candle chose that particular moment to run out of wick, leaving them in darkness.

With his face lost to the shadows, she felt Michael shift a little away from her. "Of course I don't believe in all that true love mush. I was only saying—" He rubbed one hand across his eyes in a weary gesture. "I don't know what the hell I was saying. I spout a lot of nonsense when I get tired. Would you mind if we stopped talking now and went to sleep?"

"N-no. I suppose not," she said, swallowing her disappointment.

"Good." He didn't exactly roll over and turn his back to her, but Sara could feel his retreat, even though all he did was close his eyes.

Settling back on her own pillow, she stifled a sigh. So what had she expected? Some impassioned declaration from the man? Some tender outpouring of emotion at last?

Even with what little light was left she could make out the stubborn outline of his jaw. It would take more than one night to convince him there was some magic left in the world.

Frustration with the man warred with tenderness as she pulled on the coverlets, dragging the light bedspread and sheet up to tuck them both in. Hovering over him, Sara carefully brushed back a strand of hair from his brow.

"I love you, Mike Parker. I do. So there. I think the heavens meant for us to find each other whether you believe in such things or not. Maybe I can believe enough for both of us."

She whispered the words very softly, taking care not to wake him, though she realized she needn't have worried. Even in the darkness, she could tell how exhausted the man was. She had a feeling Mike Parker had been running on empty far too long.

"Sleep, Michael," she said, pressing a soft kiss to his brow. "Because I'll be here. Catching all your bad dreams tonight."

Nine

"Good morning, Mr. Parker."

The voice was light and airy as a fairy's wings. Mike thought he must be dreaming. He was used to being awakened by the jerk in the apartment next door blasting "In-A-Gadda-Da-Vida" over his stereo or the trashmen rattling garbage cans in the alley below.

But the silvery voice came again, soft, but persistent. "*Good morning,* Michael."

Groaning, he managed to force one eye open, then the other, mere slits as he squinted against the brilliant flood of light. He seemed to be floating on some soft white cloud trimmed with eyelet and lace.

And at the foot of his cloud, haloed by sunlight stood a truly celestial being, her feminine curves undulating beneath a satin robe of shimmery blue, golden hair spilling about her shoulders. And she was holding out a cup of—

Coffee! Mike sniffed the air, a tantalizing aroma wafting to his nostrils. He must've died and gone to heaven. Better grab both the mug and the angel before somebody realized they'd made a mistake. Struggling to a sitting position, he forced his eyes open. The sunlight shifted, the angel becoming Sara smiling down at him.

Sara's face. Sara's bedroom. Sara's apartment. Memories of what had happened last night came flooding back to him with a real jolt. Perhaps because for the first time in his life, he had memories too good to be true.

She bent over him, offering him the coffee with a light kiss on his cheek. "Sorry I had to wake you, but I'll have to go out and open up the shop soon."

"That's all right," he mumbled. He accepted the cup and took a deep swallow. Hot, black and strong. Just the way he liked it. He wondered how she could have known, but he'd given up asking Sara Holyfield questions like that.

The steaming brew seemed to clear away some of the fog from his mind. He rubbed the grogginess from his eyes.

"Did you sleep well last night?" she asked.

"Yeah," he said, surprised to find that he had for a change. Deep, dreamless, secure. "What'd you do? Sprinkle some pixie dust over me?"

"Something like that." She perched on the edge of the bed with that look on her face, the expression of a woman waiting for a good-morning kiss.

He set the cup aside and obliged, pulling her down into his arms, his lips meeting hers. The kiss *did* taste of morning—warm, bright and sweet.

The woman never failed to astonish him. He didn't know what he had expected from her. A little awkwardness, embarrassment, some regret perhaps.

After all, she had wasted her first time at making love on an insensitive jerk like him. But she didn't look deflowered. She looked blooming, melting back into his embrace with an eagerness that stirred his desires to life, stronger than ever.

But it had been far easier to give in to temptation last night, caught between the mystical light of her candle and the darkness of the storm.

Mike eased her away from him. "Maybe we'd better take

these morning greetings a little slower, angel. Before things go too far.''

"Too late for that, Mike Parker," she said with a laugh, shaking her hair back.

And she was right. But in desperation, he tried again. "Sara, about what happened last night. I—"

But she placed her fingers over his lips, refusing to allow him to continue, her eyes still smiling into his. "I suppose this is the part where the hero goes all noble and tries to tell the girl how sorry he is for stealing her virtue.''

"No." Mike kissed her fingertips, moving her hand away. "Because there isn't any hero here, sugar. Just me. A first-class cynic. I was a mess last night and I took what you offered for my own selfish reasons. And I don't have the decency to be sorry about it.''

"Good, because I'm not.''

"That's because you have that misguided notion all females get, that you can take some poor slob and save him from himself, that you'll find some kind of a prince of a fellow shining underneath. Well, that won't work with me, Sara. I'm not worth the effort. You keep thinking—"

"You don't know what I'm thinking," Sara interrupted. She ran her fingers lightly, playfully down his bare chest. Mike felt his body tense in instant, eager response.

"Damn it, Sara. I'm trying to be serious.''

"So am I.''

Her hands drifted up and down the hard ridge of his rib cage, each time tracking a little lower, taunting, teasing. A half moan, half laugh escaped him. He was trying to warn her and she wasn't paying any attention to him. The blasted woman was looking at him with stars in her eyes and he feared all he'd end up doing was extinguishing them.

"God, angel, what've I done to you?''

He didn't realize he'd spoken the words aloud until Sara responded, "You made magic for me, Michael. I want you to make it again.''

Is that what she really believed? Then maybe it was up to him to show her that wasn't the case. Prove to her that there hadn't been anything magical or special about it. Prove it to himself, as well.

He caught her and flipped her back onto the bed, his kiss hard and rough. Her response was just as fierce, her tongue meeting his in a fiery dance. The two of them grappled in a heated embrace.

He tugged at the belt that held her robe, tossing it aside. Then he parted the folds, pushing them back, baring the lovely splendors of her body, naked except for the demure white silk of her panties. He ran his hands almost feverishly over her enticing curves, cupping and stroking the soft fullness of her breasts in his hands.

Sara's breath released in a sigh, her lips seeking his as she melted closer into his arms. He was never sure at what point she infused something else into their embrace, some strain of tenderness that touched him to the quick. Beauty gentling the beast. Or maybe she was simply setting him free.

He inched his fingers inside the elastic of her panties and eased them down, slipping them off so that there were no more barriers between them. His maleness pressed against the soft apex of her thighs, seeking the union they both craved.

Sara parted for him, her arms encircling him, warm and generous. She took him deep inside herself, deep into that bright warm world that seemed to be uniquely hers.

Once more there was only Sara. Her healing fire, her gentle loving. The melding of their bodies was a joyous thing, transporting Mike far beyond the shadows of his past.

It was only later when his passion had faded into a hazy afterglow that Mike's doubts returned to haunt him. He held Sara in his arms, the question she'd asked last night turning over and over in his mind.

You don't believe in love, Michael. Do you?

No, he still didn't. Did he? He wasn't so sure anymore. After all, he'd been dead wrong about one thing.

It was morning. And the magic was still there.

* * *

Sara's shop seemed destined to open late that day. It was
nearly noon by the time they made it out to her kitchen for a
bite of breakfast.

A soft summer breeze ruffled the gingham curtains and
Sara's golden curls, drawn up into a ponytail, still slightly
damp from the shower. She bustled about the kitchen humming an off-key tune as she refilled their coffee mugs.

From his perch at the kitchen table, Mike found himself
unable to keep his eyes off her, drinking in her every graceful
movement. The sweet curve of her derriere in sassy white
shorts. The soft flow of her top spangled with the signs of the
zodiac, the bright blue fabric only bringing out the brighter
blue of her eyes. Eyes still aglow from their recent lovemaking.

Mike could only watch her with a sense of amazement and
growing guilt. Amazement, because he couldn't believe it had
taken a woman as innocent as Sara to teach him more about
passion than he'd ever known in his life. Guilt, because he'd
let happen again what never should have happened in the first
place. Why did it seem like more of a sin to make love to an
angel in the daytime?

Maybe because it was harder to avoid certain realizations
with the sun glaring in your eyes. The knowledge that bedtime
magic wasn't enough to offset the kind of disagreements and
disillusionment that could spring up between a man and
woman when they weren't tangled between the sheets. His
experience with Darcy had taught him that all too well.

And there had never been two people more opposite than
himself and Sara. Despite all her exotic beliefs, Mike was fast
discovering that she was a very domestic sort of gypsy. Her
little apartment was smaller than his but it was filled with all
those woman touches—African violets on the windowsill,
cookies in the cookie jar, real napkins with a flower print, not
the kind that had been swiped from McDonald's.

All those small details that made her place into that intan-
gible something he'd never had and never would.

A home.

The thought stirred in him both a poignant longing and a

sense of deep regret. Sara drifted back across the room, setting the steaming mug down in front of him.

She settled across from him at the table, the soft fresh scent of her blending with the other aromas of her kitchen—the coffee, the fresh-baked apple-cinnamon muffins.

Mike took a sip from his cup and offered her a wry smile. He touched the T-shirt that Sara had laundered for him along with his jeans, and commented, "Clean clothes, a hot meal and a beautiful sexy dame who makes a mean cup of coffee. A guy could get used to this...."

"But?" Sara prompted, smiling at him over the rim of her cup.

"I didn't say 'but' anything."

"It was there in your voice, Michael."

He was distracted for a moment, noticing how her bangs grew more soft and golden as her hair slowly dried, tendrils escaping her ponytail to frame her face like some kind of halo.

"A guy could get used to this," he repeated with a rueful face, "but a guy like me shouldn't."

"Why not?"

"Because..." He hesitated, not wanting to hurt her, but it was far too late for him to be thinking of that now.

"Because even though what's happened between us—was something pretty spectacular, the truth is, we're two very different people, Sara."

"I noticed that." She slanted a wicked teasing glance down the length of his torso.

Great. For once he was trying to play the part of the sensible, responsible one, and Sara was cracking jokes.

Mike scowled at her. "When I leave here, you're going to go back out to your shop with its nice little healing crystals and fairy wands. But me, I'm back to hitting the streets, tracking down cheating husbands, con artists and other kinds of scum, dealing with who knows what else...."

His gaze flicked briefly to where Sara had folded his trench coat neatly over the back of his chair, the edge of that damned letter from his father visible at the top of the pocket. Like a grim shadow.

Mike looked quickly away again.

"I'm trying to warn you, angel. I'm a guy with a very uncertain future."

Sara stared thoughtfully at him. "Would you like me to rune you?"

"I already have a whole line of bank creditors willing to do that."

Sara laughed softly. "Not *ruin.* Rune. I could do a reading for you with the rune stones."

"I don't know about that—" Mike began, but Sara was already leaping eagerly up to go in search of her little rocks or whatever the hell she was talking about.

She returned quickly with a small velvet bag. She opened it to display the contents—smooth flat stones bearing weird markings on them.

"This is a practice that goes all the way back to the days of the Vikings," she said.

Mike eyed the stones warily. "No offense, Sara. But I don't think something invented by a bunch of guys who wore goofy horned hats could be that hot of an idea. If this has anything to do with predicting my future, I'd just as soon not know."

But Sara hastened to reassure him. "No. I'm not into doing fortunes like with the Tarot cards. Even I find that frightening. Rune stones are more gentle. All they do is get you in touch with your inner guide."

"Angel, my inner guide has about as much sense of direction as an old bloodhound that's lost its sense of smell." Mike gave a nervous laugh, edging his chair away from the table. This was probably all a bunch of baloney, but he'd seen Sara pull off some damned strange things. He wasn't sure he was ready for another one.

But she was giving him The Look. The big-eyed one that always melted him down like a triple-decker ice-cream cone on a hot day.

"Aw, what the hell!" he mumbled, scooting his chair back. "Go for it."

It wasn't the most encouraging request Sara had ever received, but she made the best of it. Clutching the velvet drawstring bag, she struggled to block everything else out of her mind—her own wishes, hopes and dreams. To think of nothing but Michael. His name. His image.

The stubborn beard-shadowed jaw, softened by the uncertain look to his dark brown eyes. The boyish rumple of hair at odds with the man's body poured into that T-shirt and jeans. The sexy growl morning seemed to put in his voice and—

And this was not exactly helping with her concentration.

Maybe it was safer just to think his name.

Michael. Michael. Michael, Sara chanted to herself. Closing her eyes, she reached into the bag and drew out a rune. Her fingers trembled a little when she saw what it was. The stark figure of an *X*. Maybe she hadn't done such a good job of blocking out her own wishes after all.

Mike leaned across the table to squint at the stone suspiciously. "So what's that mean? X marks the spot, like I'm going to find a treasure or something?"

"No," Sara said, feeling reluctant to tell him, anticipating his reactions. "It signifies partnership."

"Partnership?" Mike frowned. "No way, doll. I always work alone."

"There—there are other kinds of partnerships besides business ones, Michael."

There was a long painful pause and then Mike touched her hand, saying gently, "I'm sorry, angel. But I already tried that kind, too. And it was a total disaster."

That was because his ex-wife hadn't been at all right for him, Sara wanted to argue. But sometimes she wasn't sure where her psychic perceptions left off and wishful thinking began.

"Darcy and I had a lot in common," Mike continued. "If I couldn't make things work with her, I can't imagine I'd ever succeed with anyone else."

"But partnership doesn't mean thinking and acting alike. It's good for two people to remain separate and unique. The book of runes says that even people in love have to let the winds of heaven dance between them."

"In my case, it'd be more like the blasts of hell."

Sara slowly drew her hand away, wondering exactly what she was doing here. Giving Mike a reading or begging the man to fall in love with her. Either way, you couldn't convince someone of something they didn't want to believe in.

She started to put the stone back in the bag when Mike suddenly stopped her. He took the rune from her and studied it. Sara cringed, expecting some wisecrack, some jeering remark about what a load of nonsense it was.

But all he did was ask, "So you do these stone readings for other people?"

Sara nodded. "I've been pretty accurate with them or so most of my customers tell me."

"Like with your mind reading."

"Oh, I've never been real good at that, Michael, except...with you."

"So what am I thinking now?"

She glanced up and only had to meet his eyes to know. Desire mingled with deeper feelings. He wanted her in his arms, wanted to offer her things that the man, himself, didn't even know he had to give.

Without a word, Sara slipped onto his lap and wrapped her arms around his neck. He buried one hand in her hair, easing her close enough for their lips to meet. The kiss tasted of morning, bright and sweet with all its promise of a new day, new hopes and new dreams. It would have been perfect except...

Except for the constant shadow that darkened Mike's thoughts.

She drew back, stroking the hair gently back from his brow. "Don't worry, Michael," she murmured. "Whatever is in that letter from your father, I'm sure everything will turn out all right."

Mike had been hungry to kiss her again, but she felt his entire body tense beneath her, his eyes darkening with reproach.

"Sara!"

She winced. "I'm sorry. But when I touched your coat, I couldn't help sensing it was there."

"I might have known as much. There's no keeping anything back from you." He thrust her off his lap, and stood up abruptly, stalking a few paces away from her, the tender mood shattered.

Sara sighed, deeply regretting she'd said anything, certain Mike would close up on her, try to shut her out as he always did from this part of his life.

But instead, he wrenched the letter from the coat pocket and thrust it at her.

"Well, here! You might as well go ahead and read the damned thing."

Sara stared down at the envelope, stunned by the gesture, by the level of trust it implied.

"Take it," Mike snapped when she hesitated.

Her fingers closed slowly over the letter, and as soon as she did so, she shuddered. The aura was bad, very bad. One touch and she could already feel so many things, the darkness that engulfed the soul of the sender.

"Read it," Mike said. "It's really not that big of a deal."

Sara wasn't sure she wanted to, but beyond Mike's tough-guy act, his manner of hardened indifference, she could sense what he needed, wanted from her. Reassurance.

But as Sara unfolded the letter, she knew she couldn't give it to him. The words scrawled by an unsteady hand were brief and simple.

"Mikey, I'll be getting out soon. I know you haven't wanted anything to do with me and I don't blame you. But I'm asking just this once if you could come to see me before I'm released."

But it was the raw emotions bleeding beneath the pen strokes that left Sara deeply shaken.

"What are you planning to do about this?" she asked, lifting her eyes from the page.

"Ignore it." He gave an angry shrug. "Like I did all the rest of his damned letters."

"You can't this time."

"Why the hell not?"

Sara tried to find some gentle way to tell him, but there wasn't any.

"Because...because your father's dying, Michael."

"What?"

Sara swallowed and repeated, "He's dying. That—that's what he meant in the letter by getting out, being released. Permanently."

Shock and disbelief clouded Mike's eyes. "Then why didn't he just come out and say so?"

"I don't know. Maybe he didn't want to prey on your sympathy to get you to come to him."

"Oh, please!" Mike gave a snort of contempt. "If there's one thing my father is good at, that's using every trick in the book to con people into doing what he wants. If he had a card like that in his hand, he'd play it to the hilt."

"Maybe he's changed. I can feel traces of a terrible despair and regret."

"Regret for what?" Mike snatched the letter from her hand. "That he wasn't able to have me finished off? That he got caught?"

"No, I think you need to go see him, Michael, talk to him before it's too late. You said yourself that you once had doubts whether he was the one responsible for the attack on you."

"Well, I don't have them anymore." But despite his fierce declaration, there was a hint of uncertainty in his eyes. Bitterness warred against the hope of a twelve-year old boy who'd once seen his faith in his father shattered, his faith in anything good. The bitterness won out.

Mike started to tear the letter in two.

"Wait," Sara cried. "Let me hold it again. If you won't go see him, maybe I can concentrate harder—"

"No!" Mike said, shredding the paper to bits. "I shouldn't have shown it to you in the first place."

"It's all right, Michael." She laid her hand gently on his arm. "Don't you understand? You can't make love to someone without letting them get close to you."

"Why not?" he asked, tossing the remains of the letter in her trash can. "I've been doing it all my life."

He whirled around, yanking her hard against him, smothering her protest with his kiss. Trying to distract her and himself, as well.

But her words kept echoing in his head. *Your father's dying, Michael.* He didn't know if Sara could be right about that or not. But it didn't matter, because he'd closed the door on Robert Parker a long time ago. He didn't even want to think about it. He sought to kiss Sara senseless instead, focusing all his pain and confusion into a raging need.

She responded for a moment, melting against him. Then she braced her hands against his chest, seeking to put distance between them.

"Michael, please," she panted. "We've got to talk about this. I'm afraid for you."

"Don't be." He tried to silence her with another kiss, but she resisted.

"I'm afraid if you don't go and see your father now, you're going to be haunted by the shadow man for the rest of your life."

"Is that another one of your psychic predictions?" he demanded with exasperation.

Sara looked up at him with troubled eyes. "No, just something that I feel, here in my heart."

Mike flung himself away from her, raking one hand back through his hair, annoyed to find his fingers weren't as steady as they should have been.

"Listen, angel," he said. "I've got news for you. I had everything under control until you came along and started messing with my aura. I can deal with my own shadow man."

"But you haven't."

A surge of anger kicked through Mike, mostly because he knew she was right. "Anyway," he said, "it's not your problem."

"Yes, it is, because I lov—" Sara broke off what she'd been about to say, biting down on her lip. "From the very beginning, there's been some kind of strange link between us. It's what brought you to work on the case with me, searching for John Patrick and—"

"It wasn't any damned mystic link," Mike exploded. "It was a man named Storm."

"Who?" Sara asked, her brow clouding in bewilderment.

A part of Mike wanted to stop before he said something he was going to regret, something that would shatter the light in Sara's eyes. But he'd wind up disillusioning the woman sooner or later. It might as well be now.

"Storm," he repeated impatiently. "Xavier Storm, the casino king who owns half of South Jersey. You must have heard of him."

Sara slowly shook her head.

"I keep forgetting you're not from this planet," Mike muttered.

"What does this Mr. Storm have to do with anything, Michael?"

"Simple. He warned me against taking your case and he's been doing his best to make my life hell ever since."

Sara's eyes went wide. "Why would Mr. Storm do a thing like that?"

"Because for some reason he doesn't want John Patrick found. My guess is that at some point, Patrick and Storm had a run-in. Storm probably did something illegal and Patrick knows about it or—or maybe Storm even had the guy killed and his body dumped in the bay. Hell, I don't know. My detective instincts just smelled something fishy, that's all."

"And so you took the case, hoping to get justice for John Patrick?" Sara ventured.

"No!" How damn naive could the woman be?

"I took the case hoping to get revenge for Mike Parker. Storm's the guy who broke up my marriage. He seduced my ex-wife."

Sara went pale and silent at his blunt words. Then she laid her hand gently on his. "Oh, Michael. I—I'm so very sorry." Mike stifled a groan. The last thing he wanted or needed was her sympathy.

He shook her off with an impatient gesture. "So now you know why I was so anxious to solve the mystery of John Patrick. Not because of any link between us or because I felt sympathy for some dead dame who lost her son. I'm no damned hero, Sara. I don't do anything for anybody except for my own selfish reasons."

"That's not true," Sara said. "If that's what you are really like, I would have sensed it."

"Yeah? Well, maybe you're not as psychic as you think you are."

Sara flinched as though he struck her, the hurt in her eyes tearing at some place deep inside of him. He couldn't have said anything worse if he'd studied up on it for a year. Sara turned away, gripping the back of the kitchen chair, her hair veiling her face.

Mike wanted to reach out and take back his words, take her back in his arms. What the hell was he doing? Shoving away with both hands the best thing that had ever happened to him.

But he wasn't the best thing that had ever happened to her and he knew it. It would have come to this in the end. It always did with him.

Though it hurt like hell, he managed to keep his distance from her. "This John Patrick case has turned out to be nothing but a big waste of time anyway," he said. "I'm never going to find the guy."

"Are you telling me you want to quit, Michael?" Sara asked without looking at him.

"Yeah, and you should, too. Just forget about it." He swallowed thickly. "Forget about everything."

"Fine. If—if that's what you want. Just send me a bill for the days you already worked."

"There won't be any bill," Mike said, picking up his trench coat and flinging it over his arm. "I figure between all the psychic readings you've given me, we're even."

"But I didn't do a good job, Michael." Sara gave a bitter laugh. "It wasn't until now that I was able to figure out who your shadow man really is. Maybe you should go home and look in the mirror."

And she turned slowly, giving him a deep sorrowful look that Mike knew he'd remember for a long time to come. He strode toward the door while he still could, getting the hell out of there.

Long moments after Michael had gone, Sara simply stood there, her throat and eyes dry. She wasn't crying. She knew that would come later and it was going to be bad.

But for now she was taking Mike's advice. Just forget it. Forget everything. It would be a good trick if she could pull it off. Just forget the loving that had been beautiful beyond her most incredible imaginings.

Numbly she moved back to the table to clear away the coffee cups and put away her rune stones. The single stone marked *X* still lay discarded by Mike's cup.

Sara picked up the rune, cradling it in her hand. Partnership....

Maybe you're not as psychic as you think you are. Mike's harsh words seemed to whisper in her ear.

"Maybe I'm not, Mr. Parker," Sara said bleakly, dropping the stone back in the bag.

He was lost in the alley again. Mike shrank back, but this time as the shadow man stepped into the light, he was stunned to see his own face reflected back at him, glaring with menacing hate. He cried out as he took the knife and drove it into his own chest....

Dammit! Mike forced himself awake, bolting up in bed, his body soaked in a fine sheet of sweat. Through his bedroom window came the night sounds of the city, harsh and indifferent—traffic rushing, horns blaring, the shouts of a pair of drunks fighting in the street below.

It was a long way from the peace and warmth of Sara's bed. Swearing again, he shook off the last vestiges of his nightmare and dragged himself out of bed. Switching on the bare bulb that dangled above his bed, he stumbled across to a small cabinet.

Fishing out a bottle of whiskey, he poured himself a belt, letting the fiery liquid burn down his throat. Well, this was an all-time low, even for him, he thought blearily. Drinking alone, finding comfort in a bottle. Mike Parker in his skid-row-bum mode.

Glancing up, he caught sight of himself in his bathroom mirror and grimaced. Unshaven jaw, hollow, reddened eyes, straggly hair. Hell, he was the stuff nightmares were made of. He slammed the bathroom door closed, shutting out the sight.

Moving back to the bedroom, he noticed that stupid stuffed dog abandoned on a chair. It seemed to be staring at him, its single glass eye beaming a constant reproach.

"What are you looking at?" he growled.

Shoving the dog aside, he plunked down on the chair himself, placing one hand to his throbbing head. Man, for a guy who didn't believe in love, he was a real mess. These past few days since he'd last seen Sara were among the most miserable of his life, and that was saying a lot.

It was worse than when he'd found out Darcy had been cheating on him and when she'd left him. Then he'd only been in a tearing rage, hurt. Losing Sara made him feel strangely like some part had been ripped out of him. It wouldn't have surprised him at all to discover he was bleeding inside.

He'd always thought of Mike Parker as a survivor, but he'd recently recognized a self-destructive tendency in himself that he didn't like. What the hell had gotten into him? Treating Sara that way, shoving away from him with his own two hands the best thing that had ever happened to him in his life.

But that was the trouble. He obviously wasn't the best thing that had ever happened to her. He scooped up the stuffed dog and lounged back in the chair, staring at his only companion through bleak eyes.

"Sara's going to be all right. That's the important thing," he mumbled to the dog. "I'm like a bad cold, Sparky. She'll get over me in a couple of weeks."

He might have been able to convince himself of that if he hadn't made the mistake of cruising by her store today. Damned if Mike knew why he had. Nothing better to do, he guessed.

Something about her shop had disquieted him. The place had looked wrong, desolate somehow. He couldn't put his finger on it at first; then he'd realized what it was. The huge mechanical eye that had been Sara's trademark was gone.

"Aw, hell, Sparky," Mike groaned. "She took her eye down. She caved in to that Jorgensen woman and her stupid city council."

Did she? Or was it more likely Sara had caved in to Mike Parker? Who was it that had taken the biggest whack at Sara's confidence in herself?

Mike frowned, trying to dismiss the idea, but he couldn't. That eye coming down was like a symbolic gesture, that Sara no longer believed in her own unique magic, her right to be different. Or maybe she just didn't care anymore.

"Oh, God, angel," Mike murmured. "What have I done to you?" It was all right for him to be the world's biggest skeptic, but he didn't want her ending up that way. He kept having this stupid, but awful vision—Sara attending a production of Peter Pan and refusing to clap. And that damned fairy was going to die.

"I really screwed things up for her bad," Mike said. But he couldn't think of any way to put it all right again.

There is one thing you could do, stupid.

Mike scowled at Sparky. Not only was that ratty stuffed dog starting to talk back, but it was also sounding a lot like him.

"So all right, wise guy?" Mike demanded. "What am I supposed to do?"

Do what you promised to do. Find John Patrick.

"Oh, yeah, like that would really solve everything."

At least it would show Sara that you believe in her and her ghost. And maybe she'd keep believing in herself.

Mike squirmed in his seat. He hated to admit it, but the stupid dog was right.

"But how am I going to find the Patrick kid?" he asked. "I can't even find that old man Kiefer, and even if I do, there's no guarantee he'll remember anything. I've got no more leads, Sparky."

Yes, you do. A big one.

Mike stared down at the dog for a moment, thinking furiously.

"Yeah, you're right, Sparky," he said. "For a stuffed dog, you're pretty smart."

Setting the toy down, he shoved himself to his feet and made his way to the window. Even from the dump that was his apartment, Mike could see it.

In the distance, the winking lights of a millionaire's penthouse, the tallest building in Atlantic City. The home of the one man who'd held all the aces, all the answers to John Patrick's disappearance from the very beginning.

Storm.

Ten

What could a person do with a gigantic eye?

Sara stared bleakly at the mechanical contrivance that was now taking up a large portion of room on the floor of her shop. Maybe she should just dump it on Elaine Jorgensen's doorstep as a sign of her surrender. Or perhaps she could sell the thing to another business in a town with less strict codes.

Maybe an opthamologist might like to have it to advertise his profession. Or...or a private eye.

Mike's image immediately flashed into her mind.

"Oh, no, you don't." Sara pressed her fingertips to her forehead, willing the image to vanish. "Out, out! Stay out of my head!"

She'd been struggling not to think of the man for days and losing. He interfered with her concentration at every turn. She hadn't been able to do a decent reading of the runes since Mike had left. Though she wasn't sure if that was due more to a certain loss of confidence or that maybe she just didn't care anymore.

Slumping down on the stool behind the cash register, Sara let the despair sweep over her, too weak to fight it. How many lifetimes, she wondered, would it take her to get over Mike Parker? That was the trouble with being a psychic in love. You knew it was going to last forever.

Or maybe it was all just her imagination. Maybe that's all it had ever been. Her feelings for Mike, her seeing Mamie's ghost, her psychic perceptions.

Sara sighed. The phone at her elbow gave her an odd tingle. Without thinking, she answered it before it rang, just as she always did.

"Hello," she said glumly.

"Sara?" Mike's startled voice echoed from the other end.

"Michael?" she breathed. Her imagination kicked in big-time, making her feel like her heart was about to pound out of her chest with love. Just for the sound of his voice.

"Yeah, it's me," he said. "But the phone didn't even ring. How did you— Never mind. Listen, doll. Something's come up. We may be on the verge of a big breakthrough on the Patrick case."

Sara blinked. What was the man talking about?

"But Michael, you said you weren't going to work on it anymore. And besides," she added indignantly, "we're not even speaking to each other."

"Forget about that for now. I need you to get out here to the Pine Top Inn."

"What? But Mich—"

"Get out here, Sara. *Now!*"

He clicked off before she could protest, leaving her listening to nothing but a dial tone. Sara slammed down the phone, seething with frustration and anger at his presumption. Thinking that he could just walk out on her, then sweep back into her life to...

To do what? He could have given her just a hint of what was happening. Instead, she had only the sound of his voice, filling her with a vague sense of alarm.

All those psychic sensors she wasn't sure she had were going off on full alert, warning her that Mike Parker was about to do something really crazy.

Sara sped her blue compact down the dirt road, apprehension a tight knot in her chest as she worried what Mike was up to. Something rash. Something dangerous. Anything was possible with a man who'd been daring enough to confront a knife-wielding thug when he was only twelve years old.

Whatever was going on, she had a horrible fear that it was all her fault. She shouldn't have messed with Mike's aura. She shouldn't have pushed him so hard over that business with his father.

Her trepidation only increased as the old inn's towers loomed before her. Gathering dusk gave Pine Top a more sinister and threatening appearance than usual. At least, Sara thought, no matter what Mike had in mind, they wouldn't have to worry about being disturbed by Elaine Jorgensen or anyone else. No one came near the old Pine Top at night unless they were insane. Like Mike Parker.

Or herself. Sara grimaced, hitting the brakes as she pulled to a stop in front of the inn. Parked just ahead beneath the shadows of the trees were two more cars. Mike's hot red Mustang and another vehicle. Metal gray, it was one of those sleek expensive sports cars that ate up the road with a menacing purr.

Through her windshield, Sara could just make out Mike and another taller man, about a yard apart, squared off as though in confrontation. And Mike was wearing his trench coat. Mike Parker in his Sam Spade mode. Oh, dear Lord!

Shoving the car door open, Sara scrambled out, her pulse beating with alarm. She could already sense the hostility in the air. And this time it wasn't coming from the house and Mamie.

As she hurried along the drive, narrowing the distance between herself and the two men, Mike hardly glanced her way to acknowledge her approach. When she drew closer, she saw the reason for it.

Mike held a small handgun trained on the tall dark stranger.

"Mike!" Sara gasped in horror. "What—what are you doing?"

"It's called kidnapping and assault with a deadly weapon," the stranger drawled, not a small feat considering his lip was cut and swollen. "A federal offense, I believe, punishable by up-to-life imprisonment."

"Michael," Sara cried.

But Mike appeared undaunted by any possible conse-
quences of his actions. Even in the deepening twilight, Sara
could see the set of his jaw—grim, determined and…bruised.
His trench coat likewise showed evidence of a recent scuffle,
one button torn off, the sleeve smeared with blood, possibly
from the stranger's lip.

"Michael, please," Sara said. "Whatever this is about,
surely there's some better, more *legal* way—"

"I'll tell you what this about, angel," Mike interrupted.
"I'd like to introduce you to an old friend of mine. Mr. Xavier
Storm."

"—and I hate any kind of violence. It distresses my aura
and…" Sara's voice faded as the impact of Mike's words sunk
in. "Storm. You—you mean *the* Mr. Storm. The one who—"

"That's the one, doll."

Storm, the person who didn't want John Patrick found. The
ruthless tycoon that Mike suspected might even be guilty of
his murder.

Sara stole a nervous glance at the man with the lean, arrogant features and night black hair. A handsome man, exuding
a dangerous kind of sensuality and power despite the fact his
expensively tailored suit was streaked with dust, his tie yanked
askew.

Studying Sara from beneath hooded eyes, he said, "So you
must be Parker's client, the woman who runs the New Age
shop. You'll forgive me if I don't offer to shake hands, Miss
Holyfield, but…" He raised his arms slightly and Sara saw
that Storm's wrists were manacled together. Good God, Mike
had the man handcuffed.

Sara was appalled and somewhat relieved. She could feel
something very dark emanating from Xavier Storm. Something dark and frightening. Shivering, she drew back closer to
Mike.

"Michael, I don't understand. What…how did this happen?
I mean how did Mr. Storm end up…"

"Being knocked down, handcuffed and held at gunpoint by
a lunatic who thinks he's Humphrey Bogart?" Storm filled in,
managing to sound amazingly bored with the entire situation.
"Just my lucky night, I guess."

Mike glared at him. "It all happened quite simply, Sara. I told Storm I had evidence regarding what had become of John Patrick, and if he didn't meet me out here alone, I was going public with my information. As soon as he realized I was bluffing, things got a little...tense."

A little tense? Despite Storm's relaxed manner and Mike's deadly calm, there were enough undercurrents crackling between these two men to have exploded Newark. Sara glanced from one to the other with increasing dismay.

This was like a scene out of one of Mike's steamy detective novels or those old grainy black-and-white movies he liked to watch. Only, this was horribly real.

"Please, Mike," Sara said, plucking nervously at his sleeve. "Whatever you think Mr. Storm has done, let the police handle it."

"Oh, I think the police are the last people Parker would want to see just now," Storm said with a sneer.

"Or just put the gun away and—and let him go."

"Let him go?" Mike echoed in disbelief.

"The lady shows some common sense, Parker," Storm said. "Amazing. Who would ever expect it from a client of yours?"

Mike glared at him while growling at Sara. "Don't you understand, angel? This is the guy who can solve your case for you. He can tell you what happened to John Patrick."

"I don't care," Sara said miserably, her head crowded with visions of Mike being carted off to prison for assaulting, or God forbid, maybe even shooting this Xavier Storm. "Why are you doing this? You told me you didn't give a damn about John Patrick anymore, that you wanted to drop the whole thing."

Mike compressed his lips in a stubborn line. "I never quit any case until it's finished."

"Oh, I think I can give you a better answer than that," Storm purred. "The man's finally gone round the bend, Miss Holyfield. Do you know what he muttered during the course of our—er—negotiations here tonight? He has some peculiar notion of what will happen if he doesn't solve this case for you. Something to do with fairies."

"What?" Sara frowned in confusion.

"Shut up, Storm," Mike said, making a menacing movement with the gun.

But Storm continued to address his remarks to Sara, unperturbed by Mike's glare. "He said something about being afraid if you lost faith, the next time you wouldn't clap, either, and the fairy would die."

"Don't pay any attention to him, Sara," Mike said. "He hit his head when I knocked him down."

"I'd say it was the other way around." Storm's tone clearly expressed what he thought of Mike's sanity but his revelation had other implications for Sara. Her gaze flew to Mike's face. She could see him turning red, even in the fading light.

"Michael, did you really say that?"

"So what if I did?" he shot back.

"And you did all this, took this terrible risk, for me?"

Mike shrugged, trying to put on his gruff look. "After the way I upset you the other day, I couldn't leave you doubting yourself, maybe even ending up as cynical as me someday. I had to find some way to show that—that I do believe in you, Sara."

"So you decided to solve the Patrick case by kidnapping Mr. Storm? All so I'd get my faith back. Oh, Michael." Sara found it hard to swallow, moved to the point of tears. "I th-think this is most wonderful thing anyone's ever done for me."

Oblivious to the gun, to Storm, to everything, Sara flung her arms around Mike's neck. Mike gathered her close with his free hand, still managing to keep the weapon trained on Storm.

Sara buried her face against his shoulder. "Oh, Michael, I'm so sorry. Our quarrel that day was my fault. I was being so unreasonable. I didn't mean to push you into anything like this."

"It's okay, gypsy lady. Don't go getting all weepy on me. Everything's going to be all right." Mike brushed a light kiss against her hair. "Don't you know I'd risk anything to keep the stars in your eyes?"

Beautiful words, incredible words coming from Mike Parker. Sara lifted her face to his but the tender moment was shattered by Storm's mocking voice.

"How touching. Maybe the judge will assign Miss Holy-field a cell next to yours, Parker. Padded, of course."

"You just leave Sara out of this. She has nothing to do with my assault on you."

"She does now. However, I'm a reasonable man, Parker. Put the gun away, unlock these cuffs, give me back my car keys and I might be persuaded to forget this whole unpleasant episode."

"Do it, Michael," Sara urged. "I appreciate what you tried to do for me. For Mamie. But just let him go. You're never going to force anything out of him with that."

"Don't worry about the gun, doll. It's not even loaded," Mike whispered. "It's not me that can get the information. It's you."

"Me?" Sara echoed, startled. Maybe Mike had lost his mind. "How?"

"Just touch him. Read his aura or his thoughts or whatever that thing is you do."

Dear heavens. Was the man serious? Sara stole a frightened glance at Storm's sinister countenance and shook her head. "I c-can't."

"Don't be afraid. I won't let him hurt you."

"It's not that, Michael," she faltered. "It's just...I'm not sure that it would work. That I really can—"

"You've got to try, Sara. It's our only shot. I believe you can do it."

She searched his eyes and saw incredibly that he did. The belief was there—warm, fierce and strong. It made her want to fling herself into Mike's arms all over again.

But she turned, trembling, to face Xavier Storm. Hugging Mike's encouragement close to her heart, she took a few steps closer to his prisoner. Storm watched her approach through wary, sardonic eyes.

"M-Mr. Storm. Would you mind if—if I touched your hand?"

Both of his arrogant dark eyebrows shot upward in surprise. But he gave a faint shrug. "Be my guest. I've never had any objections to being touched by a beautiful woman."

Mike scowled. Hovering close to Sara's side, he hissed in

her ear. "Don't go stirring up his aura the way you do mine. Just suck out his memories. That's all."

"Michael, please," Sara murmured. This was nerve-racking enough without him barking out instructions. Taking a deep breath, she reached out, closing her hand over Storm's. He had long, surprisingly sensitive fingers for a man, very graceful, very elegant and very cold.

He started a little at her touch and Mike snapped, "No false moves, Storm, or I'll scatter your brains all over that fancy suit of yours."

"Michael!" Sara protested. "I can't concentrate with—the threat of violence in the air. Are you sure that thing's not loaded?"

Mike shot her a blistering look, but Storm laughed, a sound of genuine amusement.

"Never mind," Mike said, brandishing the gun. "I can still use it to bash in your head."

But Storm ignored him, his mocking gaze focused uncomfortably on Sara. He was taking full advantage of the situation, engulfing her fingers in his, lightly stroking, able to infuse an alarming amount of smoldering sensuality into the simple contact. Sara was glad of Mike's strong presence at her elbow, glad she wasn't anywhere on her own with the dangerous Mr. Storm.

But beneath the man's arrogance, his pose of assured power, ruthlessness, Sara was beginning to pick up on other things. Buried deep. Fear, the dread of being alone, unending despair.

Sara shivered as she felt herself being pulled farther into the dark world of Xavier Storm. Deep into his soul, a wasteland where there was...nothing. Only an emptiness as bleak as looking on the face of death itself.

An image came to her, a terrible vision of Storm sitting behind an expensive mahogany desk, papers scattered about, a gun held in his shaking hands as he sought for the courage to pull the trigger.

Her startled gaze flew to his face, and suddenly the tall, proud man before her began to dwindle, smaller and smaller, changing shape to become a little boy clutching a ragged dog—lost, scared and alone. Forever alone.

Sara's fingers tightened around Storm's. As the face of the

boy melted back into the man's gaunt features, Sara gazed up at him, her eyes blurred with tears.

"John Patrick," she whispered. "Welcome home."

The electricity had been turned off at the Pine Top Inn after Mamie had frightened off the last batch of workmen and Elaine Jorgensen had had trouble finding another crew. But Sara always seemed able to come up with a supply of candles.

She lit several in the cobweb-festooned dining room, the candlelight reflecting a soft glow on Sara's face. Whatever happened to him as a result of this crazy night's work, Mike thought, it would be worth it just to have the shine back in her eyes. Even if he ended up doing life.

Did people get life for kidnapping in New Jersey? Mike wondered uneasily. In his case, Storm would probably demand the death penalty.

Mike glanced to where he now had the casino king hand-cuffed to a chair, the tycoon's eye swelling to match his lip. Storm had made rather violent objections to being escorted into the inn.

Or should Mike say John Patrick?

"I still can hardly believe it," Mike muttered to Sara. "That that bastard Storm could turn out to be that cute little kid in all Mamie's pictures."

"Why?" Sara asked. "Because you dislike Mr. Storm so much, you were sure he had to be some kind of desperate villain or murderer?"

"Yeah. Partly that, and well...." Mike rubbed the bridge of his nose and confessed sheepishly. "This case has been so strange from the very beginning, so many coincidences between Mamie's story and my own mother's...that there was a moment when I wondered...I almost feared John Patrick might turn out to be me."

"Oh, Michael." Sara laid her hand gently on his cheek.

"Hey, it's okay," he said briskly. "I'm not disappointed or anything. I'd rather think my mother is at peace instead of off haunting somewhere. But this leaves us with a big problem, angel. What are we going to do about him?"

"I don't know," Sara said, her gaze tracking ruefully toward their sullen prisoner.

"I mean I was kind of counting on you picking out some incriminating evidence from Storm's brain so we could haul his butt off to the police. Instead, I'm afraid it's going to be the other way around."

Mike's eyes roved around the eerily silent inn. "I never thought I'd be looking to a ghost for rescue, but you don't suppose Mamie could put in a good word for us."

Sara fretted her lower lip. "I don't think Mamie is here, Michael. I'm not sensing her presence at all."

"What! I thought you said she couldn't go anywhere else."

"I didn't think that she could," Sara lowered her eyes and said in a small voice. "But after we had our quarrel, I came out here to see her one last time. I told her you'd quit the case and didn't think John Patrick could be found. I—I am afraid she may have given up and gone away."

"Oh, great! The woman haunts this blasted old inn for years and she picks tonight of all nights to turn in her ghost union card." Mike groaned, raking his hand back through his hair, realizing the full desperation of the situation they were in. The situation *he* had put Sara in.

"We're in big trouble here, angel," he said, wearing a path in the dust-covered floor. "Storm is going see us both fried for this. Mamie's little son Johnny has grown up to be a real vindictive man."

"He's grown up to be a very troubled man," Sara said softly. "I know why Mamie was so worried about him. His soul is ashes, Michael. I had this vision of him sitting at his desk the other night. He—he was trying to work up the courage to kill himself."

"Storm?" Mike cast a startled glance toward where his prisoner sat lost in the shadows of the dining room. "I thought he'd be rich enough to live forever."

"He's the poorest man I've ever met."

Mike continued to eye Storm doubtfully. "Well, whether that's true or not, I guess all we can do is try to get the guy to admit that he's John Patrick. It's the only chance we've got."

He strode over to where Storm lounged in his chair, trying

to maintain a pose of impatient boredom. But the casino king's eyes flicked around the inn walls and Mike caught a glimpse of emotions he knew all too well.

The ragged look of a man confronted by his past, raked over by a thousand painful memories. Mike had never expected that it would be possible that he'd feel a twinge of sympathy for Storm. But he did and it irritated him.

"All right," Mike said, planting himself in front of the man. "You might as well come clean. If Sara says you're John Patrick, then that's who you are."

Storm affected a yawn. "I guess I should be grateful she doesn't think I'm the White Rabbit."

"Please, Mr. Storm." Sara crept up to stand beside Mike. "I mean...John. Your mother has been worried about you."

"My mother is currently sunning herself on the Riviera," Storm drawled. "And she never worried about me a day in her life."

"I mean your real mother. Mamie Patrick."

Storm's lips thinned. "Never heard of her."

"Yeah?" Mike asked. "And I suppose you don't recognize her, either."

Mike pulled Mamie's little jewel case out of his trench coat pocket and plunked in on the table before Storm. He spread out the photographs, drawing particular attention to the one of Mamie with her son hiding behind her skirts.

Something flickered briefly in Storm's eyes. Then he hunched one shoulder. "A rather dreary little collection. If you're going to bore me with family photographs, Parker, don't you have anything more interesting?"

"How about this?" Mike produced Sparky and plunked him down on the table. It was a desperate ploy and Mike didn't really expect it to have any more effect than the pictures.

But Storm looked stunned and then mumbled, "It—it's Blinkey."

"Blinkey?" Mike said. "What the hell kind of name is that for a dog?"

"Michael, shh!" Sara cautioned, gesturing toward Storm. An odd change shifted over the man's hard features, a softer light stealing into his intense eyes as he regarded the stuffed toy.

"Where—where did you find this?" he asked hoarsely.

"Right where you hid it so long ago. Beneath the floorboard in your mother's closet. Don't you remember?" Sara prompted when Storm hesitated. "You were afraid the toy was going to be thrown away by the man who came to take you away from the inn. You called him the gray man. You were afraid of him."

Storm compressed his lips, lapsing into stony silence, refusing to say anything more.

Mike heaved a long sigh. "There's only one thing to do. We've got to get Mamie back here, Sara. Can't you hold a séance or something?"

"I—I don't know," she whispered, casting a nervous look at Storm. "I guess I can try to call her."

Picking up a candle, Sara paced to the center of the room, the tiny flame casting an eerie glow up over Sara's solemn features.

"Mamie?" she said tentatively. "Mamie, please. We've found your son for you."

Storm squirmed in his chair, glaring up at Mike. "What the hell are you trying to do here, Parker? This—this is really sick, even for you."

"Just be quiet and wait," Mike snapped.

Sara drifted around the room, holding the candle up, peering hopefully into every shadow. "Mamie, John Patrick is here now and—and he needs you desperately."

Storm became more agitated, tugging uselessly at the cuffs binding him to the chair. "Damn it, Parker! All right, the bloody woman was my mother. She sold me off when I was five years old. Are you satisfied? Now can we end this farce?"

Sara turned back to Storm, looking horrified. "Sold you off? Who told you such a terrible thing?"

"My stepmother did," Storm said with a bitter twist of his lips. "She never let me forget it. Eloise was always too happy to remind me of how my father, Alexander, got some stupid backwoods girl pregnant. When he later discovered that he couldn't father any more children to carry on his name, he tracked down Mamie Patrick and bought back his son."

"Damn!" Mike exchanged a startled glance with Sara. "So

the mysterious gray man wasn't anyone from child welfare, but John Patrick's own father.''

''Perhaps he was, but the rest of what Eloise Storm said isn't true.'' Sara turned gently back to Storm. ''Don't you see? When your father did finally return to claim you, he couldn't have bought you from Mamie because she was already dead by then.''

''It makes no difference now.'' Storm's brief flare of anger died, the dull light creeping back into his eyes. ''Now I've told what you wanted to know. Why don't you just let me out of here? There's going to be a lot of investment brokers and bankers distressed by my absence.''

But no one else. Storm's sense of isolation, of being unloved was as apparent as if he'd spoken it aloud. It was an odd feeling to Mike—being able to get so tight inside the guy's skin.

Maybe because it was right where he had been himself. Before Sara. Hardly knowing what he was doing or why, Mike found himself stalking over to the steps leading up from the lobby and bellowing, ''All right, Mamie. Damn it, get down here now or there's gonna be hell to pay. Enough of these tricks. You wanted me to find your kid and I got him here. If you don't show up, I'm gonna start making so many spook cracks, your ears will burn.''

Mike's words rang up the stairs, echoing to silence.

''That's it, Parker,'' Storm said tersely. ''This is your last chance. Let me go now and I'll forget—''

Storm's words were drowned out by the sudden slamming of a door. The door to the dining room began to bang violently open and closed. The chandelier shook and trembled.

Mike caught his breath, a sudden blast of cold air striking his chest, shoving him back from the stairs.

''Mike,'' Sara cried, clutching at his hand to steady him.

The chilling wind tore through the room, all but extinguishing the candles. In the next instant, a blinding white light appeared on the stairs.

Mike squinted, clinging to Sara. He shielded his eyes with one hand, frozen with disbelief. In the middle of the glow, he could see a form emerging, delicate, almost transparent. The form of a wistful young woman wearing a pleated skirt and soft sweater, her dark hair drawn up in a ponytail.

"Mamie," Mike said in hushed tones.

The apparition paused at the foot of the stairs and raised one hand beckoning. Mike was so mesmerized he would have stumbled forward to follow, but Sara held him back.

"No, Michael. It isn't either of us she wants." She nodded toward where Storm sat, looking as dumbstruck as though he'd turned to stone.

There was a chink of metal and the handcuffs that held him to the chair came miraculously undone, falling to the floor. Rubbing his wrists, he stood up slowly. When the ghost beckoned again, he moved like a man in a trance, brushing past Sara and Mike without appearing to see them.

Storm trailed after the spirit of Mamie Patrick, and the pair of them vanished into the darkness at the top of the stairs. Silence settled over the room once more and Mike Parker finally remembered to breathe.

He glanced down to find Sara looking as awestruck as he felt.

"You know," Mike confessed, swallowing hard, "until the moment Mamie actually appeared, I—I still wasn't sure I believed she was real."

"Neither was I," Sara said with a tremulous smile. Flinging her arms around Mike, she buried her face in his shoulder.

It was one of the strangest, most wonderful nights Mike thought he'd ever spent. Sitting on one of the dusty settees in the lobby with Sara cradled in his arms, waiting for Xavier Storm to finish meeting with the ghost upstairs.

He'd heard of men experiencing an apocryphal moment in their lives, but of course he'd never believed in such a thing. Funny what it had taken to fling the doors of his mind wide open to any possibility, any sense of wonder. The appearance of a ghost, his old enemy Storm and a certain gypsy lady.

Mike gazed down tenderly to where Sara was curled up against his chest. He dropped a kiss on top of her golden head and murmured, "I love you, Sara."

She'd fallen asleep and didn't hear him, but that was okay. He'd have plenty of time to tell her. For the moment, it was enough for him just to realize it, to feel something in his heart besides the emptiness and doubt that had been there for so long. Mike drew Sara closer against him. Resting his head on top of hers, he closed his eyes....

The next time he opened them, he was surprised to see the soft light of morning spilling across the inn floor. He stirred, wincing at the stiffness in his back and neck. His movement, slight as it was, disturbed Sara. She sat up, yawning and rubbing her eyes.

"Goodness. What—what time is it?" she mumbled.

What time was it? For a moment, Mike wasn't even sure where he was. Then memories of the night before came flooding back to him.

The ghost of Mamie Patrick. Storm... Storm? Mike straightened, glancing quickly around him, but there was still no sign of the casino king.

Mike bolted to his feet, a moment of raw panic setting in. What if Storm had crept out and gone for the police after all? Or worse still, what if Mamie had decided to put her kid out of his misery and take him with her? How were Mike and Sara ever going to explain away Storm's dead body?

But before he could alarm Sara with any of these possibilities, Mike heard a light step on the stairs. Spinning around, he saw Storm descending to the lobby and he breathed a sigh of relief.

He studied Storm critically, not quite sure what he expected to see. His hair turned white or a glazed look to his eyes. But the casino king appeared remarkably calm for a man who'd just spent the night in the company of his dead mother.

"Good morning," Storm said softly with only a trace of his old irony.

"Good morning," Sara replied, but Mike didn't feel up to any social amenities. There were at least a dozen questions he wanted to put to Storm about what had happened last night. But Storm strode right up to Sara and took her hand.

Mike had never seen Storm at a loss for words, but the tycoon hesitated before saying, "For the past few weeks, I've been cursing you, Miss Holyfield, without even knowing who you were. Only knowing you were the person responsible for dredging up things I wanted to forget. Now I just want you to know that...that I'm grateful to you for...for helping *her* to find me.''

"You're welcome, John," Sara said, smiling shyly up at him. "But you have Michael to thank for getting you here last night."

"Yes," Storm said dryly, touching his bruised eye. "Thanks a lot, Parker."

"No problem." Mike grinned. "Just as long as you show your gratitude by not sending for the cops."

"I'll make a deal with you. I won't send for the cops if you don't send for the press. I've seen enough of my private life splashed across the tabloids over recent years."

"Of course we wouldn't," Sara said. "That wasn't what this was all about."

"Thank you." Storm carried Sara's hand to his lips. Not one of his usual smooth gestures, but something more genuine. "I take it that I'm now free to leave?"

The last question was addressed more to Mike. He stepped aside, sweeping Storm toward the door with a mock gallant bow. As the man left the inn, Mike hastened after him, following him to his car.

"Here's your keys, Storm," he said. "And I thought you'd probably want to have this, too." He held out the small box containing Mamie's cache of treasures and photographs.

Storm looked at the small case for a moment. Then he accepted it, a softened look coming into his eyes.

"Thank you," he said.

"And...you better have this, too." Mike was embarrassed to find that it cost him a pang as he handed over the ragged stuffed dog.

Storm looked equally embarrassed and gruff about receiving it, but he tucked the dog along with the box carefully inside his car. He started to slide into the front seat of the Jaguar himself when he paused.

His eyes flicked uncertainly to Mike and then he blurted out, "For what it's worth, Parker, I never slept with your wife. Her real lover was a lounge lizard who worked at my casino."

Mike stared at him. "Why the hell didn't you ever tell me that before?"

"You never gave me the chance. Besides, I'm used to people thinking the worst of me. I rarely stoop to defend myself."

Mike was shaken to discover how well he understood Storm's attitude. It was so close to his own.

"Well, thanks for setting things straight," Mike said. "But whatever happened with Darcy, it's not important anymore."

"I would imagine it isn't," Storm replied. "You're a very fortunate man, Parker, to have found someone like Miss Holyfield. A woman you can love enough to risk everything for."

A pensive look crossed Storm's face. If it had been anyone else besides the mighty casino king, Mike would have said the man appeared damned wistful.

Storm made another movement to leave, but this time it was Mike who stopped him. "Listen, I know it's none of my business, Storm, but something like we all experienced here last night doesn't happen every day. Your mother...Mamie. Did she say anything? What did she want from you?"

Storm's face went still. He was silent a moment before replying.

"Only to see if I was all right. To tell me how sorry she was that she hadn't been able to take better care of me. To make sure that I knew how much she really did love me."

"Oh." Mike said softly.

Storm slid behind the wheel of his car. Mike stepped back, only vaguely aware of the man starting up the Jaguar. His thoughts had suddenly been yanked far away. To an old man dying in a state prison.

When he snapped out of his reverie, Storm's car was vanishing down the drive and once more Mike was struck by some of the parallels between Storm's life and his. His bitterest enemy. So very different. So much the same. If he wasn't careful, he might end up actually liking the guy, and Mike had suffered enough shocks to his system for one day.

Turning, he made his way slowly back to the inn. Sara stood in the middle of the great dining room, holding out her hands as though she would catch the sunbeams melting through the tall glass windows.

"Can you feel it?" she asked spinning toward Mike, smiling. "The whole aura of peace. Mamie is at rest."

"Yeah," Mike agreed, but all he could feel was the effect

Sara was having on him, watching the sun turn her hair to gold, the dream-spun look in her blue eyes.

"You must be feeling pretty good too, gypsy lady. Vindicated at last."

"I felt vindicated long before Mamie showed up. The moment that I realized you believed in me enough to risk everything."

Mike paced over to her, coming to a halt bare inches away. He shoved his hands awkwardly in his jeans pockets.

"I love you, you know," he said gruffly.

"I was beginning to suspect as much," she said. "But it's awfully good to hear it."

He held out his arms and she moved into them, close to his heart right where she belonged. Their lips met in a tender kiss that was full of all the tender things he needed to tell her but didn't yet know how to say.

There was so much to be settled between them, but there was one thing that needed to be taken care of first. Sara had been right all along about so many things.

Mike had a long journey to make. Up north to the city of Trenton. To confront his shadow man one last time.

Eleven

The old Pine Top ballroom gleamed with the soft white glow of electricity emanating from the newly refurbished chandelier. The walls smelled of fresh paint and polished woodwork, all hint of ghosts and memories swept away.

Elaine Jorgensen had done a phenomenal job whipping the inn into shape for the Last Rose of Summer dinner dance, but Sara found herself missing the old atmosphere of dust and cobwebs. All the building's aura and personality seemed to have vanished with Mamie.

Sara lingered by the tall glass windows, wistfully watching the couples dancing on the lawn outside beneath colored lanterns, the lilting music from the band drifting through the open casement. Her strapless tea-length gown of shimmering white silk rustled about her knees as she tapped one toe in time to the music. Both the night and the dress whispered of romance, the stuff fairy tales and dreams were made of.

There was only one thing missing, Sara thought ruefully. Her escort. She hadn't heard anything from Mike for weeks. She could do nothing but wait and worry, missing him, hoping his painful journey into his past was going well for him.

Sara understood completely why he'd forgotten about the dance. She'd almost decided not to attend herself, but Mike's words kept coming back to her. *"You don't want to let the wicked stepmother win, do you, Cinderella?"*

So she'd come alone, but defiantly, her head held high. It's what Mike Parker would've expected of his woman...though Sara was not entirely sure she was his. So much had been left unsaid between them, the future unsettled. If there really was going to be any kind of future for the two of them.

"Sara, my dear. You look very nice tonight." Elaine Jorgensen's cool voice broke in on Sara's thoughts.

Sara turned reluctantly to face the older woman. Ever since dinner had ended, Elaine had been making her circulation of the room, greeting guests like a grand duchess. Evidently, she decided even Sara must have her turn.

"I'm so glad you were able to come," Elaine said with her familiar brittle smile.

Yeah, about as glad as a nudist facing a swarm of mosquitoes. The unexpected quip popped into Sara's head in a very Mike-like tone of voice. Dear God, she was starting to think like the man.

Choking back a sudden urge to laugh, Sara managed to thank Elaine and make some vague and polite remark about how well the inn looked.

"Yes," Elaine agreed complacently with another flash of her teeth. "I wish I could say the same for your shop, dear. You had the good taste to take that dreadful mechanical eye down for a while. But now you've had the thing stuck back up again."

"Yes," Sara said with a breezy shrug. "I changed my mind."

Elaine's smile faded. "I thought I made myself clear on this matter. I would be loathe to do so, but if you don't have that monstrosity removed, I'm going to have to file a complaint."

"Then you'll have to file it with the attorney I've hired."

"I'm very disappointed by your attitude, Sara. I suppose we will end up in court."

"I suppose we will, Elaine. But you won't win."

"Good Lord!"

At first Sara thought it was her manner of supreme confidence that provoked this reaction from Elaine, but then she saw the woman's eyes directed toward the entrance to the ballroom. As were every one else's in the room, twisting to gape at a late arrival.

Turning herself, Sara uttered a soft exclamation and forgot to breathe.

Mike Parker paused beneath the archway, sporting a black tux and elegant white bow tie. The clothing molded to his tall frame, emphasizing his broad shoulders and lean waist, making him appear suave, sexy and dangerous. A tawny-haired lion springing up to startle a roomful of awestricken does. No other man in the room had troubled to dress so formal; no other man looked so devastatingly handsome.

Mike's dark eyes raked the room until he found Sara. Totally oblivious to the sensation he was causing, he strode purposefully in her direction.

Sara's heart pounded hard enough to rival the orchestra's drummer. Fifty years from now and she had a premonition that Mike Parker was always going to make her feel this way when he entered a room.

He paused barely a hand's reach away from her, his mouth tipping into that familiar quirky smile.

"Hello, angel. Sorry I'm late."

"It's all right, Michael," she murmured. Everything was more than all right now.

Sara gazed up at his face, drinking in the sight of him, feeling as though they were the only two people in the room. It came as a shock to hear Elaine's voice at her elbow.

"This is a private party, young man. By invitation only."

"It's okay, Mrs. Jorgensen," Sara murmured. "Mr. Parker is my guest."

"He wasn't listed when you finally turned in your reservation. Late I might add. So I'm going to have to insist—"

"Go to hell, Elaine," Sara said, her eyes never leaving Mike's.

"What?" Elaine gasped.

"Go to hell," Sara repeated sweetly. "Please."

Mike choked on a laugh. After sputtering incoherently for a moment, Mrs. Jorgensen spun on her heel and stalked off.

Mike's eyes twinkled down at Sara. "I don't think I've ever seen that done quite so politely."

"There's never any excuse for abandoning good manners, Michael."

"Like I did. I've kind of left you hanging these past few weeks and I'm sorry for it. You must have thought I forgot all about tonight."

"I'm just glad you're here now."

"Me, too." Both his eyes and his voice seemed to caress her, sending a shiver along her bare shoulders. "You look good, Sara. Real good."

"So do you."

"Yeah, Mike Parker in his Prince Charming mode." He flicked the lapel of his tux with a self-deprecating grimace. "But you better come dance with me before I turn back into a toad."

Reaching for her hand, he swept her outside onto the lawn—and into his arms. The band had struck up a love song, smoky and slow.

Mike held her close to him, resting his cheek next to her temple. Although they had never danced together before, Sara found no difficulty matching his step, her body, her rhythm fitting perfectly with his.

"It feels so good having you back in my arms," he murmured close to her ear. "I missed you, gypsy lady."

"I missed you." Sara nestled close to him with a contented sigh. She didn't want to raise any shadows to shatter the mood, but she had to know.

"Did—did you see your father? Is everything all right?" she asked, tipping up her face to his.

"He died five days ago," Mike replied softly.

"Oh, Michael, I'm so sorry."

"Yeah. So am I." Mike swallowed, straining her closer. "But I did get there in time to spend a lot of time with him in the prison hospital. Funny thing, angel. I spent most of my life hating him, turning him into the monster in my dreams. And when I got there, he was just this frail old man."

"Were you able to talk to him at all?"

Mike nodded. "I don't believe anymore that he was behind the attack on me that night. He finally talked to me about my mother, too. He gave me a photograph of her. And a name. Marie.''

"That's a lovely name, Michael."

"After she died, my father said he simply didn't know what to do with me. He'd never been much of a family man, but I suppose in his own way he did care about me. Did the best he could. I was able to forgive him, but—''

Mike's jaw steeled with determination. "But I'll do a lot better by my own kids. If I ever have any that is.''

"Two boys and a girl," Sara blurted out.

When Mike stared at her, her face flushed bright red. "I— I mean, if I was ever going to have a family, that's what I'd have."

He smiled at her and their steps slowed, out of sync with the orchestra, hardly moving at all. Sara looked deep in Mike's eyes and found something new there. A hard won sense of peace.

And something old. A tenderness that had always existed just beneath the surface, but now he was no longer ashamed to show it. He stopped moving altogether. Taking her by the hand, he led her away from the lawn until they stood secluded from the lights and the music.

Gathering both her hands into his, Mike said, "I've been having dreams again, angel.''

"So have I," she whispered.

"Good ones, I hope?''

She nodded, but she hardly dared tell him what they were. She didn't have to because Mike said, "I dreamed you were all in white with your hair hanging down the way it is now. And we were in this dinky little chapel with stained-glass windows...."

"That spilled rainbows of light on the pews, and the minister had a bristly gray mustache..." Sara added.

"And I slipped this old-fashioned ring on your finger."

"A lover's knot of gold fashioned like vines and roses," Sara finished.

A silence fell over them, no longer stunned, but both a little awed by this magic they shared.

Then Mike cleared his throat. "So do you think it's possible that dreams can predict the future?''

"I think anything is possible, Michael."

"And that if we looked for it, we'd really find a chapel like that?"

"I wouldn't be at all surprised."

"Neither would I. Because I found this in a little antique shop in Trenton." Fishing around in his inner pocket, Mike produced a small tissue-wrapped parcel. He undid the wrapping to reveal a delicate ring, roses and vines wrought in gold. The exact same as in the dream.

"Can I try in on you for size? That is do you think that a gypsy lady like you and a mug like me could ever—I mean, Sara that—" Mike broke off with a groan. "Hell, I was a lot more smooth about this in the dream. What I'm trying to ask you is—

"Yes!" Sara cried.

Mike grinned. "You know, sometimes it's a handy thing a woman being able to read your mind."

Her fingers trembled a little when he slipped the ring in place, her heart full to overflowing. But when he gathered her into his arms, her response was strong and steady, her lips meeting his in a passionate kiss where past, present and future all seemed to blend as one.

Breathless moments later, Mike said hesitantly, "This is going to sound really strange, Sara. But I keep having this feeling we've done this all many times before."

"You mean you're starting to believe in reincarnation?"

"Hell, no. That is I'm not sure." His eyes became solemn and serious. "The truth is, Sara, I don't know if my mind will ever be able to be quite as open as yours. If I'll be able to believe in all the things you do.

"But what I do believe is that I love you. And you love me. And it's going to last forever. Is that enough?"

"Oh, yes, Michael," Sara said, gazing tenderly up at him. "More than enough for one lifetime."

*　*　*　*　*

In April 1997
Bestselling Author

DALLAS SCHULZE

takes her Family Circle series to new heights with

TESSA'S CHILD

In April 1997 Dallas Schulze brings readers a
brand-new, longer, out-of-series title featuring the
characters from her popular Family Circle miniseries.

When rancher Keefe Walker found Tessa Wyndham he
knew that she needed a man's protection—she was
pregnant, alone and on the run from a heartless past.
Keefe was also hiding from a dark past...but in one
overwhelming moment he and Tessa forged a family
bond that could never be broken.

Available in April wherever books are sold.

Take 4 bestselling love stories FREE

Plus get a FREE surprise gift!

National Bestselling Author

MARY LYNN BAXTER

"Ms. Baxter's writing...strikes every chord within the
female spirit."   —Sandra Brown

LONE STAR
Heat

SHE is Juliana Reed, a prominent broadcast journalist whose
television show is about to be syndicated. Until the murder...

HE is Gates O'Brien, a high-ranking member of the
Texas Rangers, determined to forget about his ex-wife. He's
onto something bad...

Juliana and Gates are ex-spouses, unwillingly involved in an
explosive circle of political corruption, blackmail and murder.

In order to survive, they must overcome the pain of the past...and
the very demons that drove them apart.

Available in September 1997 at your favorite retail outlet.

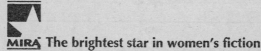

MIRA The brightest star in women's fiction   MMLBLSH

Look us up on-line at:http://www.romance.net

As seen on TV!
Free Gift Offer

With a Free Gift proof-of-purchase from any Silhouette® book,
you can receive a beautiful cubic zirconia pendant.

This gorgeous marquise-shaped stone is a genuine cubic
zirconia—accented by an 18" gold tone necklace.

(Approximate retail value $19.95)

Send for yours today...
compliments of 🌹 *Silhouette*®
™

To receive your free gift, a cubic zirconia pendant, send us one original proof-of-
purchase, photocopies not accepted, from the back of any Silhouette Romance™,
Silhouette Desire®, Silhouette Special Edition®, Silhouette Intimate Moments®
or Silhouette Yours Truly™ title available in February, March and April at your favorite
retail outlet, together with the Free Gift Certificate, plus a check or money order for
$1.65 u.s./$2.15 can. (do not send cash) to cover postage and handling, payable
to Silhouette Free Gift Offer. We will send you the specified gift. Allow 6 to 8 weeks for
delivery. Offer good until April 30, 1997 or while quantities last. Offer valid in the
U.S. and Canada only.

Free Gift Certificate

Name: _____

Address: _____

City: _____ State/Province: _____ Zip/Postal Code: _____

Mail this certificate, one proof-of-purchase and a check or money order for postage
and handling to: SILHOUETTE FREE GIFT OFFER 1997. In the U.S.: 3010 Walden
Avenue, P.O. Box 9077, Buffalo NY 14269-9077. In Canada: P.O. Box 613, Fort Erie,
Ontario L2Z 5X3.

FREE GIFT OFFER   084-KFD
ONE PROOF-OF-PURCHASE
To collect your fabulous FREE GIFT, a cubic zirconia pendant, you must include this
original proof-of-purchase for each gift with the properly completed Free Gift Certificate.

084-KFD

IN CELEBRATION OF MOTHER'S DAY, JOIN
SILHOUETTE THIS MAY AS WE BRING YOU

a funny thing

HAPPENED ON THE WAY TO THE

DELIVERY ROOM

THESE THREE STORIES, CELEBRATING THE
LIGHTER SIDE OF MOTHERHOOD, ARE
WRITTEN BY YOUR FAVORITE AUTHORS:

KASEY MICHAELS
KATHLEEN EAGLE
EMILIE RICHARDS

When three couples make the trip to the delivery
room, they get more than their own bundles of
joy...they get the promise of love!

Available this May,
wherever Silhouette books are sold.

Silhouette®